ID955630

The Women Who Walk

THE WOMEN who WALK

Stories by

Nancy Huddleston Packer

LOUISIANA STATE UNIVERSITY PRESS
Baton Rouge and London
1989

Copyright © 1962, 1976, 1981, 1982, 1983, 1985, 1989 by
Nancy Huddleston Packer
All rights reserved
Manufactured in the United States of America

First Printing
98 97 96 95 94 93 92 91 90 89   5 4 3 2 1

Designer: Sylvia Malik Loftin
Typeface: Caledonia
Typesetter: G & S Typesetters, Inc.
Printer: Thomson-Shore, Inc.
Binder: John H. Dekker & Sons, Inc.

Library of Congress Cataloging-in-Publication Data

Packer, Nancy Huddleston.
    The women who walk : stories / by Nancy Huddleston Packer.
        p.   cm.
    ISBN 0-8071-1458-8 (alk. paper)
    I. Title.
    PS3566.A318W66   1989
    813'.54—dc19   88-28617
                                                    CIP

    The author gratefully acknowledges the Associated Students of Stanford University and the editors of *Greensboro Review, San Francisco Review, Sequoia,* and *Threepenny Review,* in which some of these stories previously appeared.
    "Breathing Space" and "Homecoming" first appeared in *Sewanee Review,* 90 and 91 (Spring, 1982, and Fall, 1983). Copyright © 1982, 1983 by Nancy Huddleston Packer. Reprinted by permission of the editor.
    Stories that first appeared in *Southwest Review* are reprinted by permission of the editor. They are "Lousy Moments" (Spring, 1976); "The Women Who Walk" (Winter, 1980); "The Day the Tree Fell Down" (Summer, 1982); and "Making Amends" (Winter, 1985). Copyright © 1976, 1980, 1982, 1985 by Nancy Huddleston Packer.

    The paper in this book meets the guidelines for permanence and durability of the Committee on Production Guidelines for Book Longevity of the Council on Library Resources. ∞

For Ann Packer
and George Packer

Contents

The Women Who Walk

Breathing Space

Claire slips the gray silk dress over her head. She hears the clang of a pan dropped into the stainless steel sink in the kitchen below her bedroom. She opens her jewelry case and chooses the aquamarine bracelet Victor gave her last Christmas. She hears utensils falling against the pan and into the sink. She gathers her keys, a small handbag, a cashmere shawl to ward off the early autumn chill. More utensils are dropped. Would a glass now be thrown? Would there be a cut finger? Blood? Quickly she leaves the room and walks down the carpeted stairs and into the kitchen.

Lucy's thin little body is bent over the sink, resting on her forearms. She is staring out the window at their patch of Bay Bridge in the distance. Apparently she has not heard Claire. Claire thinks her way through several possibilities. I hope your lamb chop wasn't overdone. Was the bus very crowded? Your father will be here in half an hour.

"Well, darling," she begins in a carefully light, cheerful tone.

Lucy spins around and water sloshes down the front of her jeans. At fourteen she looks eleven, and yet her expression now, her expression so frequently, is pinched and hostile. She looks Claire up and down, up and down. A little grin creeps around her mouth. Claire waits. Claire is what Dr. Stringfellow calls "taking it."

"Oh, Mummy darling," says Lucy in her sweet-sarcastic voice, "looking so pretty for what lucky man tonight? Victor? Or somebody else's husband?"

Claire forces a self-mocking smile. If Lucy needs these little attacks, let her have them. Claire sits down at the kitchen table. She knows that if she appears in a hurry, Lucy will

1

make a scene. "Your father will be here soon," she says. Lucy has left the boarding school across the Bay without permission, and Phil has agreed to drive her back that evening.

Lucy says, "I'm not going back." Suddenly her face unclenches. She catches her lower lip between her teeth and appeals to Claire with her eyes. "Don't make me. Please, Mother."

When Lucy looks like that, sad and innocent, like a waif, Claire feels the solidity seeping from her bones. She feels she cannot resist Lucy. She thinks, Yes, it would be all right for Lucy to stay this once. But then she reminds herself that Dr. Stringfellow does not want her to give in to Lucy's appeals. Giving in is bad for Lucy. She sighs and shakes her head. "They said if you get back before lights out, there wouldn't be any punishment this time."

Lucy's expression shuts down and she looks fierce again. "Lucky me," she says. "No water torture. No bamboo under the fingernails."

Claire says, "No losing your right to go downtown in the afternoon with your friends."

"They never invite me to go with them," says Lucy. "They hate me, as usual."

Claire feels the fall of anxiety through her chest. "It just takes time," she says, but she does not wait for Lucy to dispute that with a list of failures. "Anyway, no losing your telephone privileges." Lucy frequently telephones Claire from a pay phone down the corridor from her room at the dorm. These calls—full of complaints, threats, sometimes tears—are very painful to Claire, but she believes that they help Lucy. They are Lucy's safety valve. She says, "I'd miss our phone talks."

"At least you could drive me. It'll only take an hour."

"I told you—I have a dinner date I can't break."

"Victor Christos," says Lucy, nodding.

"No, a couple from St. Louis, ready to close on a three-hundred-thousand-dollar condo. I do have to make a living, you know. Anyway, Phil wants to see you."

"He'll probably be drunk," says Lucy.

2

"He'll be all right," says Claire. At six o'clock, when Claire asked Phil to drive Lucy back, he was all right—cleansed, he assured her in his teasing way, of the detritus of alcohol by a day out-of-doors with his flowers. Phil was trained as a landscape architect, but now he is little more than a gardener, talented and charming enough to compensate, almost, for being unreliable. But Phil is reliable when it comes to taking care of Lucy. She tries to think of something to make going back easier for Lucy. "Hey, you didn't tell me about that English essay you were having such fun writing. How'd it turn out?"

Lucy lowers her head. "That turkey they call an English teacher marked off a whole grade just because I spilled a little orange juice on my paper."

Claire thinks that Lucy no doubt spilled a lot of orange juice, deliberately, testing the teacher. "Well, she may not like . . ." Claire stops and changes direction. "She's probably allergic to oranges. She's probably all broken out in welts by now."

Lucy's face lights up and she giggles. Lucy is so pretty when she laughs, so fresh-looking and open. Claire walks over to her and drops her wrists across Lucy's thin shoulders. Lucy leans her head on Claire's arm. It is a nice moment. They have so few these days, these years. "The turkey will probably be on cortisone for six months," Claire says. With her free hand she brushes the bangs from Lucy's forehead, and as she does her cuff slides back. Without thinking, she glances at her wristwatch. It is eight-fifteen. She told Victor she would meet him no later than eight-thirty. "I mean, how would you like it if you looked like a big red balloon for six months?"

Lucy's gaze has followed Claire's. She jerks away. "You don't care about me at all!" she shouts. "You just want me out of your way."

Heat rises into Claire's face. She wants to turn and leave, but she must stand without flinching, absorbing Lucy's message of sudden hate. After a moment she says, "I care, I care desperately. If I didn't care, would I take this?"

Abruptly Lucy says, "Want to know what I wrote my essay on?" She looks a little smug, a little mean. Claire does not want to know about the essay, but she nods. "It was supposed

3

to be something unusual that had happened to you. So I wrote about this." She runs her right index finger over the little scar on the underside of her left wrist. She laughs. "The orange juice was because I couldn't find any tomato juice. I wanted it to be realistic."

Claire feels a stab of pain in her groin. Lucy in the bathroom, the red pooling in her palm, spilling into the porcelain basin, the ride to the hospital, the stitches, and Lucy grinning and grimacing in turn.

It was a bluff, of course. Dr. Stringfellow, the psychiatrist Claire consulted, pointed out that the wound was slight, little more than a nick that a few stitches took care of. Lucy, Dr. Stringfellow said, would never really hurt herself. She was just expressing anger, perhaps because of her sense of failure at the public high school. Dr. Stringfellow said Lucy needed a fresh start, and he recommended the school across the Bay. Claire is one of the leading brokers at Victor's firm, and she can pay the high price of the fresh start.

At first Lucy was all for it, but after only a few weeks she has soured on it and now feels hostile and hurt. She wants to quit. Claire says she has to stick it out for the first term.

Dr. Stringfellow agrees, saying, "Anyway, you both need a little breathing space."

"Want to read it?" asks Lucy. "It's very graphic." She smiles at Claire. One of her cunning smiles.

"I'll forego that pleasure," says Claire. She notices a dirty paper napkin on the floor, and she picks it up and carries it to the trash basket. She doesn't want Lucy to tell anyone at school about that night. She is afraid it will make Lucy's relations with the other girls more difficult. She is afraid the school authorities will use any pretext—Lucy's coming home without permission, for example—to get rid of Lucy. She wants Lucy to have the fresh start. She wants breathing space.

Claire says, "If you're ready to talk about all that, perhaps you ought to start with Dr. Stringfellow."

"That stupe," sneers Lucy. "He's a jerk. You're wasting your money making me go to him."

4

"It's not a waste if it's helpful," Claire says.

Lucy narrows her eyes until only slits of light are visible. She says, "What is it you think is wrong with me anyway?"

"Nothing is *wrong* with you," says Claire. She walks over to Lucy and leans down so that their faces are close. "I just want you to be . . . happier." Even to herself her voice sounds wheedling and false. Lucy stares at her, her face stark, no longer a waif.

"Then leave me alone!" shouts Lucy, twisting away. "Then I'll be happier." She stalks out of the room and up the stairs.

Claire checks the range and oven to be sure they are off. She squeezes a stream of detergent into the pans and fills them with hot water. As she opens the front door, she hears a sound from upstairs. She pauses. Is it Lucy calling her? Then she sees Phil's old Ford Fiesta turning the corner. She closes the door and hurries down the short flight of stairs to the sidewalk. When she returns later that night, Lucy will be gone, the house at peace, reclaimed.

She walks down the half-dozen blocks to the little out-of-the-way Italian restaurant where she and Victor can count on not being seen by anyone they know. Claire had once been friends with Victor's wife, Beth. Occasionally Lucy played with their child, Lisa. But ever since Claire and Victor became lovers, over a year ago, the two women have not seen each other. Claire knows that Beth knows, but Victor doesn't discuss one woman with the other. Sometimes Claire misses Beth, but these once-a-week meetings are her happiest times.

The owner and the waiter nod to her, and she sees Victor sitting at the corner table. He stands as she approaches. He is blond and boyish-looking, but he plays this down by dressing in dark conservative clothes. When he slips the shawl from her shoulders, he kisses the top of her head. "You look wonderful," he says.

As she sits down, an immense sigh breaks up through her chest. She has not realized how tense she is. "What?" asks Victor.

5

"What else?" says Claire, shrugging. "I wonder if I could have a martini five minutes ago."

Victor's eyes track the waiter, who turns instantly, as though touched. Waiters seem always to turn at a glance from Victor. Victor orders a martini over ice for Claire and asks for the menus. "Poor Claire," he says. "And of course poor Lucy. Poor teenagers."

Claire shakes her head. "If only it were just being a teen-ager." Perhaps she should have gone back when she heard Lucy calling. So often after an outburst Lucy won't speak to her for days, savoring her fury and triumph. Did Lucy have something special to tell her this time?

The waiter puts down the martini and Claire reaches for it. Victor puts his hand around hers on the martini glass. "I love you," he says. "I hate to see you worried."

Claire smiles, breathes deeply, carefully relaxes her shoul-ders. "When I'm with you, I'm a lot better," she says.

During dinner they are colleagues. That property, that sale, that possibility. It makes them laugh to remember that they became lovers over a business deal, when they had trav-eled together to New York. She tells him she has the St. Louis couple *sur le point.* He says she is marvelous. He has always admired her. She can take care of herself. And of Lucy. And, God, for how many years of Phil, too.

He puts his hand on her thigh. "I've missed you," he says. Last week Victor and Beth went to Los Angeles for a cousin's wedding.

Phil. Suppose he was already drinking when she called. She feels tricked by Phil, by herself. Angrily she says, "You've been on a short leash." Victor removes his hand. When she sees the boyish hurt on his face, she is sorry. "Joke," she says. "Misfired." She grins at him and taps her shoe against his. "I don't want any dessert, do you?" He smiles and calls for the check, and the waiter brings it at once.

The phone begins to ring as soon as they enter the house. Lucy is safe. Or is it Lucy? Victor puts his hand on the back of

Claire's neck and shakes his head. She runs into the kitchen and picks up the phone.

The operator says, "I have a collect call . . ."

"I'll accept it," says Claire. "Lucy? Everything okay?"

"Cool. Neat. Groovy. If you don't count Phil trying to do figure eights in the middle of the bridge."

"Was he drunk?" Claire asks. Victor stares at her in disbelief. Victor is solid, reliable, not like Phil.

"You didn't plan to get rid of both of us in one blow, right in the middle of the Bay, did you?" Claire waits. She knows from Lucy's voice that Phil was all right, but she wants Lucy to say so. "Okay, so he wasn't drunk, but you weren't positive, were you?"

"I know you're angry with me for making you go back," says Claire, "but I'll make it up at Thanksgiving. We'll have five days together."

"Golly. Gee. Wow," says Lucy. "Five whole days with Mummy."

"We'll go to Tahoe, or Carmel." Thanksgiving. It is a bleak time. Victor will take Beth and Lisa to their place in Mendocino. Other friends will put on or go to large family dinners. Claire's only brother lives in Pennsylvania. Last Thanksgiving she took Lucy to Trader Vic's for a special treat, but Lucy refused to order anything. "Maybe L.A. It'll just be the two of us," she says.

"No Victor Christos slipping in and out of bed among other things late at night when I'm supposed to be asleep?" Lucy hardly pauses. "He's there right this minute, isn't he?"

"I told you I had a St. Louis couple closing on a condo." Claire feels herself smiling. Lucy is so intuitive and full of quick perceptions. Claire turns to Victor. "What a kid," she mouths. Victor just shakes his head. He is leaning against the oven with his arms crossed. "I'm too tired to fence with you tonight, darling," Claire says into the telephone. "We can talk tomorrow."

Quickly Lucy says, "The door to this prison must be made of solid concrete. Want to know why I think so?"

7

Claire sighs. There is no way she won't be told. "You tried to kick it in when they locked it after Phil let you off." It was hardly a guess. Kicking at doors is not new. Lucy once put her foot through the hollow-core door of her bedroom. When was that? Was that when the little boy next door wouldn't let her come in his house? "Was anyone around?"

"Don't worry. The old lady had gone back to her room. I almost broke my leg. I just thought you'd like to know there's maximum security at this prison for loony rich kids."

"You're not loony, and I'm not rich."

"Then why do I have to stay here?" asks Lucy triumphantly.

Claire repeats what she has said often before. "Dr. String-fellow wants you to get a fresh start, and he thinks it would be good for both of us to have a little breathing space." Victor taps his wristwatch with his forefinger and walks out into the hall. Once Lucy talked for a half hour, with Victor pacing the floor. Finally he had switched on the television.

Claire now says, "Anyway, we can talk about all this tomorrow, when I'm not so tired." Through the doorway she sees Victor starting up the stairs. "I'm going to hang up now." As she hangs up, she hears Lucy shout "Go to hell!"

Claire walks into the bedroom. Victor puts his arms around her. "Bad?" he asks.

Claire shrugs. "Normal. Usual. Awful." For an instant she is sorry she said this, sorry she betrayed Lucy.

"Poor baby," says Victor. He begins to kiss her face. The telephone rings.

Victor's eyes flare. "This is too much," he says. "Please don't answer it." He stares at Claire. She nods.

As they undress, as they slip beneath the silk sheets, as they begin to touch each other, the telephone continues to ring. "You really should do something about her," Victor murmurs into Claire's ear. Claire controls her urge to laugh, to say, Oh what a brilliant suggestion.

Soon the rhythm of his body and the sound of his blood seem to drown out the ringing of the telphone, and Victor's face takes on its soft yet intent look. Claire forces her body

8

into the motions of giving pleasure, the motions of receiving pleasure. She thinks that perhaps she should have answered the telephone. She imagines Lucy's face, the lower lip caught between her teeth, her eyes wide and bare. But Dr. Stringfellow wants her to resist Lucy's demands. Only then will Lucy break that terrible clutching dependence. Lucy, Claire thinks, must be forced to assume responsibility for herself. Victor says, "Now. Yes," and she realizes the telephone has stopped ringing.

After a while, Victor sits up on the edge of the bed and says, "I have a feeling your heart wasn't in it."

"How could it be?" she answers. "I am her mother. Suppose it were Lisa." Asking for it, she knows. She hasn't long to wait.

"Beth wouldn't tolerate that for an instant—that kind of utter selfishness." He leans down and draws on his dark socks. She feels distaste rise into her throat. It seems vulgar, almost immoral, to have on socks when the rest of him is naked.

He stands up and begins to put on his clothes. As he buttons his shirt, he turns to face her. "I'm sorry," he says. "That was dumb and cruel and insensitive, and I'm sorry."

She stares behind him at the wall. "Not important," she says.

He stuffs his shirt into his trousers. "It's just that I'm worried about you. You've got to stop letting her beat on you this way. It isn't good for her or you. And to be honest, I have to admit it's sort of getting to me. Getting between us, I mean. Perhaps . . ." He pauses as he reaches for his shoes.

She says, "Perhaps we ought to put this little affair on hold until all this blows over?"

"Don't put words in my mouth," he says, frowning. Even so, she thinks that she has probably only been taking the words out. "I was going to say perhaps you could tell the school not to let her call."

"At least not when you're here," she says.

The look on his face indicates that he can't decide whether to get angry or ignore her remark. She is goading him, testing him. Finally he says, "I don't seem to have a comb. May I bor-

9

row this?" He picks up her big-toothed pink comb and runs it through his hair.

"Perhaps all this will never blow over," she says. "Perhaps this is the way it's going to be." She watches as he knots his tie and slips into his jacket. "Affairs blow over, as clever wives know, but, alas, a child goes on forever."

He comes to the side of the bed. "I know you're upset," he says, stroking her cheek and temple, "but don't ruin what we have."

Suddenly she finds herself clinging to him. He is what she has, brings joy and warmth to her. She loves him, his kindness, even his loyalty to Beth.

"Next time I'll unplug the phone," she says into his shoulder. "Promise."

She listens to the sounds of his departure. The clicks as he turns off the hall lights, the muffled thud as he closes the front door and then tries it from the outside to be sure, the revving of his car engine. She clicks off the bedside lamp.

The telephone is ringing and it is Dr. Stringfellow and he is saying that Lucy has tried to kill herself and they have put a straitjacket on her and Lucy is screaming Mother Mother come get me and Victor is shaking his head and saying that Lucy and Lisa can never play together again.

Claire breaks from sleep and fumbles for the telephone. Has she been dreaming? Did she actually speak to Dr. Stringfellow? Where is Lucy?

"I have a collect call to anyone . . ." begins the operator.

"It's just me," says Lucy, and Claire says, "I'll take it." She sits up on the edge of the bed and looks at the luminescent hands of the clock. It is nearly four. "This finishes it," she says into the telephone. "I won't tolerate your selfishness any more. You've got to stop beating on me like this."

"Please don't scold me," says Lucy in a quiet voice.

"No wonder you're having trouble there, waking everyone up in the middle of the night. What must the other girls think of you. My God, what do you think of yourself?"

10

"Not very much," says Lucy. "Come get me. I'm afraid."

"Ah, a new twist," says Claire. "And just what are you afraid of? Some big mean girl down the hall?"

"After you wouldn't answer the phone, I tried to go to sleep, I really did. But I kept thinking I was going to get up and kill myself."

Again Claire feels the stab of pain in her groin, but then she remembers that Dr. Stringfellow warned her that Lucy would probably say something like this. "God, Lucy," she says. "You'll stop at nothing."

"I kept seeing this terrible picture. I'm in the bathroom down the corridor, standing at the second basin, and I see myself slicing my wrist. The blood . . . Please come and get me."

"I can't take it anymore," says Claire. She is cold, and she reaches for her dressing gown on the chair beside the bed. "From now on when you feel the overpowering need to beat up on someone, call your father for a change—he ought to be sober by four A.M. Or call Dr. Stringfellow—I pay him enough." She shrugs into the dressing gown.

"I'm sorry," says Lucy. "I know I'm terrible. But please."

"No," says Claire. "You've got to take more responsibility for yourself. You've got to get over this dependence of yours."

Now she waits for the sudden rage, shouting, tears. "Lucy?" she asks. She realizes the line has gone dead.

Claire switches off the light and lies back against the pillows. She feels exhausted, and yet she knows sleep will be a long time returning. She will look a mess tomorrow when she meets the St. Louis couple. Lucy knows exactly how to inflict maximum damage.

Even as she thinks this, Claire knows that Lucy is the damaged one. Although she has gotten progressively worse, there was always something wrong with her. Claire remembers the first time she faced that, when Lucy was four. She remembers Lucy throwing herself down the short flight of steps after the cat, pell-mell, heedless, shrieking. Claire remembers when Lucy ran away and spent the night in the public toilet of the neighborhood park, all alone. Lucy was seven then. How gray and fierce and silent she was when the policemen finally found her and brought her home the next day. Even now, Claire feels panic when she thinks about that public toilet. And sometimes Claire thinks that Phil's drinking got out of control beginning then.

Claire thinks about all the doctors she has consulted over the years—the pediatricians, the psychiatrists, the endocrinologists, the nutritionists. None has ever satisfactorily explained Lucy, not even the famous ones from Cal and Stanford. One doctor thought there might be a chemical imbalance, but wasn't sure. One diagnosed a kind of childhood schizophrenia that perhaps Lucy would outgrow. Another said Claire's long unhappiness with Phil could be expressing itself through Lucy, that trying to keep her marriage together for Lucy's sake was exactly wrong. But divorcing Phil hadn't helped—it only added fuel to Lucy's fury.

What is it? Claire wonders, lying in the dark. Is it blood? Vitamins? An unfortunate mix of genes? Is it me? She has tried to be a good mother. She has tried to do her best. You do this, you do that. But though you cause, you can't control the consequences. You damage, even when you try not to.

She turns on her side and closes her eyes. Now she tries a trick she once learned, of consciously relaxing each muscle of her body, one at a time. She starts with her big toe and then her little toes and the side of her foot and heel. Oh, your toe bone's connected to your ankle bone, oh, hear the word of the Lord.

She remembers that she and Phil used to sing that song to Lucy as they bathed her in the kitchen sink when she was a baby. They sang and wiggled her toes and her heel and on up her body, and she had laughed and wanted more more more. Claire remembers the sound of that laughter, like a little chirp. She remembers the baby smell. And that sets off a long chain of memories. Lucy's little shell-like ears. Lucy climbing into the double bed on Sunday mornings, and the warmth of her little rag-doll body. She even remembers that after the fiasco at Trader Vic's they went to Ghirardelli Square and Lucy

12

ate an immense hot-fudge sundae and then tried to lick the chocolate off her cheeks and chin, and they both laughed until they almost cried. Claire realizes that not all the memories are wretched and painful. Wonderful ones are massed on the edge of her awareness, waiting, ready, forward, receding, indelible. So many that there must be little room for anyone else.

Claire wonders what she will remember of Victor once their affair is on permanent hold. The way he commands waiters? His socks? His kindness? She knows she will lose him soon. He will never leave Beth. Claire knows she is only a way-station on his long journey of infidelity. She remembers how furious Lucy was when she discovered the affair. Isn't he Lisa's father? she asked. That's dumb. But at least he doesn't wear Nikes and sweat suits, she said, and at least he doesn't boss me around. Some lover had worn Nikes, some lover had bossed Lucy.

Claire sits up. Has Lucy turned off the burner? The oven? She gets out of bed and goes downstairs. When she sees the pan in the sink, she remembers that she has already checked the kitchen. Just a free-floating uneasiness, perhaps because Lucy hasn't called back. She picks up the kitchen telephone. She will dial the number of the pay phone in Lucy's corridor, but she will only let it ring once. That way she won't wake anyone, but Lucy will know she called.

When she gets the busy signal, she thinks Lucy is trying to call her. She hangs up and waits. She looks out the kitchen window at the lights on the Bay Bridge. She remembers Lucy's dull voice. That isn't like her. Lucy is manic, tense, shrill. Claire goes to the sink and scrubs the pans and puts them to dry on the drainboard rack. She goes back to the telephone and dials again. Again she gets the busy signal. At four-thirty? Perhaps Lucy is talking to Phil, telling him about her fantasy of killing herself. Poor Phil, already sinking under his massive burden of guilt and shame.

Dr. Stringfellow says not to worry about Lucy's threats, not to make too much of them. He says Lucy is one of those who will never do it. How does he know? By what magic can he peer into the mystery of Lucy's mind? Is his opinion based on statistics? Of x-number of teenagers who try suicide, only one succeeds? How do they know which one?

Claire dials Phil's number. The telephone rings once and she hangs up. Lucy is not talking to Phil. As Claire starts up the stairs, she thinks that Lucy has deliberately left the phone off the hook so that Claire could not call back.

At the top of the stairs Claire's gaze strays toward Lucy's room and then toward the bathroom. It is all before her now. She sees the phone hanging dead alongside the box. She sees Lucy walk down the darkened dormitory corridor and into the large bright bathroom. She sees her stand before the second sink. She sees the razor. And she understands why Lucy does not want the dorm alerted. Lucy is not bluffing. She is the one statistic who will.

Suddenly Claire is panting. She feels as though her heart has sprung loose in her chest. But she knows she must not give in. She must find help. She runs into her room and picks up the telephone.

No one will be in the school office at this hour, but there is a telephone in the housemother's apartment downstairs from Lucy's room. Claire tries to remember the woman's name. Something with B. Two syllables. She thinks of Dr. String-fellow, but he lives twenty miles down the Peninsula. She dials Phil's number and the phone rings and rings. No doubt Phil is drunk.

She decides to call Victor. It has been over a year since she has spoken to Beth and she no longer remembers the number. She flips the flimsy pages of the telephone directory until she finds Christos. She dials. In a sleep-heavy voice Beth says, "Yes? Who is it?" Of course, the telephone is on Beth's side of the bed. Claire hangs up.

She dials 911. A man with a young voice asks for her name, address, telephone number, and the nature of the problem. When Claire says her daughter is in school, he asks if she is locked inside? Claire explains that Lucy lives there and that the school is across the Bay. The man says that is in a different jurisdiction and Claire should call . . . Claire flings the telephone into the cradle. It is up to her.

She slips off her dressing gown and quickly puts on slacks and a sweater. She thrusts her feet into loafers and grabs the cashmere shawl she has carelessly hung over the doorknob. She starts down the stairs. So many times she has imagined her life without Lucy, without the pain of Lucy. And now that obscene secret wish is coming true. She will have her life without Lucy. Her legs melt beneath her. She half-falls down the last two steps and grabs the stair post to catch herself. Harsh animal howls break from her. Her throat is clogged with noise and she feels that she is suffocating.

When she hears the ringing of the telephone, she stops keening. She begins to breathe again. She thinks she will let the telephone ring. She will be as cruel as Lucy, inflict as much pain as she can. She imagines Lucy standing at the pay telephone waiting, waiting alone in the dark corridor. Claire runs into the kitchen and picks up the telephone. "I'll accept it," she says before the operator can speak.

"Hello, Mummy darling," says Lucy.

The Women Who Walk

In the days right after Malcolm left her, Marian began to notice the women who walked the deserted streets near the university campus. They were a flash of color in the brilliant June sunlight at a distant intersection, a single shape thrusting through the shadows of the giant sycamores along the sidewalk. She did not at first differentiate one from another. She was too absorbed in her own suffering. Images of Malcolm that last day spun through her mind. The thin ankle over the thin knee as he sat on his luggage in the front hall. The silver lighter touched to the black cigarette. Well, Marian, he said. She pulled the car over to the curb and gave herself up to the blurring tears, the sudden thunder in her chest.

Soon, quieter, she looked around the empty street. Had anyone seen her? She saw in the distance a lonely figure, walking, walking.

Two weeks had passed, and she had not yet told the children. She had said, "He's out of town, he's at a conference, he's giving a lecture, he'll be back." One evening as they sat in the dying sun in the patio, Joseph, who was eleven, said,

"When? When will he be back?"

A bluebird squawked in the high branches of the silver maple. "Your father . . ." She began. She felt suffocated by the heat in her throat. Molly began to cry and buried her face in Marian's lap. His face suddenly flaming, Joseph ran into the house. Later that night, Marian called Malcolm at the backstreet hotel where he had taken a room. "I can't tell them," she managed to say and quickly hung up.

Next day, Malcolm carried the children away for lunch.

After that, each evening he spoke to them on the telephone. On the following Saturday, he took Joseph to a Giants game. On Sunday, he and Molly visited a horse farm in the hills. Marian longed to know what he had said, whether he had spoken of her. But they did not tell her.

Finally she asked. Molly grew somber, hooded, afraid. Joseph became moody and glared at the floor. Molly said,

"Daddy says we're not to carry tales back and forth."

"You're my children," she said.

"His, too," said Joseph, "just as much as yours."

She felt an explosion and a wind and a fire, but she sat silent and staring.

The first few weeks, women she had counted as friends called her on the telephone, invited her to lunch, came to visit. From behind the living-room curtain, she saw them walk up the drive, often in tennis whites, practicing an overhead slam or a low backhand as they waited for her to answer their knock. When she opened the door, their faces were grave. They sat on the sofa and rested their sneakers against the coffee table and frowned and shook their heads in sympathy.

She could not speak of him. She tried to talk of other things, but all paths through her mind led back to the injustice she had suffered, of which she could not speak. The silence soon weighed too heavily on them, and their faces grew round and flat as moons, and pale. They knew they could not help her. They must leave now, they said, but they would return. They wished her well. They were her friends. She heard their tires sighing as they escaped down the street.

They were not her friends. They were the wives of his friends, the mothers of his children's friends, the neighbors who were no more than friends of his house. She had no friends. She would never be able to speak of herself, to share herself with friends. He had exiled her to an island of silence. She stood up and began to move around the room, shifting ash trays, picking lint from the floor. She felt a restless, angry energy gathering in her.

17

During the summer, Marian frequently saw the woman in the large black coat walking rapidly on the outskirts of the university or the residential streets bordering the business area of the town. She thought the woman was an older faculty wife who apparently spent her leisure doing good works, carrying petitions door-to-door or collecting for the Cancer Society or the Red Cross.

The woman wore sandals and heavy dark socks, a floppy straw hat and the black coat. The coat was shaped like a wigwam, with sloping shoulders and a wide skirt that struck her just above the ankles. Marian thought the woman wore it like a burnoose, protection against the dog-day heat of August and September. The woman was obviously a character, a throwback to the days when faculty and faculty wives were rather expected to be eccentric. Marian liked her, liked her independence and freedom from vanity. Often Marian waved as she drove by, but the woman never seemed to see her. She kept her eyes down, as if she were afraid she might stumble as she rushed along in her waddling, slue-footed gait.

One hot day in late September as Marian waited for a stoplight, the women in the black coat started across the street in front of the car. Marian had never seen her close up before. She was much younger than she looked from a distance, about thirty-five or so, Marian's age. And still quite pretty, with a high-bridged, delicate nose and delicate fine lips, and a soft-looking pale skin. When she came even with the front of the car, she abruptly twisted her head and glanced at Marian through the windshield. As their gazes met, Marian knew that she had seen the woman before—how long ago, under what circumstances she could not recall, perhaps at a university party, a meeting, at the sandbox or the swings of the city park. She would never forget those startled pale gray eyes.

Marian waved but the woman ducked her head again and hurried on to the sidewalk. Watching her—the hunched tension of her neck and shoulders, the awkward, powerful, rushing gait—Marian felt that when they had met, they had been drawn together in one of those rare moments of intense though

18

inexplicable intimacy. And now Marian longed to recapture the strange, treasured feeling.

She drove around the block and pulled into a driveway in the woman's path. She got out and stood leaning on the fender, waiting, smiling. The woman walked straight at her, heedless, but at the last moment, without lifting her gaze from the ground, veered clumsily aside. Marian reached out and touched her shoulder. "Wait," she said. "Don't I know you?"

The woman stopped and after a long moment lifted her head. Her gaze whipped from Marian to the sky to the trees. She pulled her coat collar up around her face. Marian said, "What is it? Can I help you?"

The woman threw back her head, like a colt shying, and opened her mouth. Marian heard the sound—distant, muted—of a strangled voice, and she thought the voice said, "I'm so very cold." For an instant the woman stared at Marian, but then she lowered her head and rushed down the street.

Malcolm came late one evening to settle details. He sat in the red leather chair he had always sat in. He looked handsome, tanned, his graying hair tousled and longer than he had ever worn it. When he asked how everything was, he was charming and attentive, his smile warm and pleasing, as if she were his dinner partner. She sat on the edge of the wing chair, her knees close, her hands kneading each other, and told him the lie he wanted to hear. Yes, everything was fine. He nodded at her approvingly, no longer angry and irritated with her.

"Well, now," he began, and leaned forward. She did not want to hear it all just then, and she stood up.

"I'll get some coffee," she said. "Turkish coffee," she pleaded. He sighed and nodded.

She went into the kitchen and turned on the faucet. She waited for her heartbeat to slow. When she heard his footsteps, she busied herself with cups and saucers. He stood in the doorway and gazed around him, smiling at the wall decorated with dinner plates from different countries.

"I always liked that one," he said, pointing to a Mexican

19

plate he had brought to her from Mexico City where he had gone for a conference. But, he hastened to assure her, she needn't worry, all he wanted were a few mementos, keepsakes that had been in his family for a long time. The tintype of his great-grandmother and of course its antique frame and the silver ladle his great-great-aunt had saved from the Yankees. He smiled. Everything else was hers, absolutely, he didn't want anything else. Nothing.

Nothing? she wanted to ask. Nothing? No memento, no keepsake of our fifteen years together?

"Nothing besides coffee?" she asked. "Some fruit?" She picked up an immense pineapple from the straw basket on the counter. It was ripe, soft and yellow. He had always loved pineapples. "It's just ripe," she said. "I'll cut it for you." When he shook his head, she held it close to his face. "Smell it," she pleaded.

"I do not want to smell it, for God's sake," he said. For an instant, his composure dropped away and she saw what she had remembered all these months—the rigid shoulders, the pinched mouth, the hard, irritated eyes. She could easily drag the sharp points of the pineapple across his face. She watched little specks of blood ooze from his skin, swell into a long thick ruby stream that marked his cheek like a savage decoration. She put the pineapple down and handed him a cup of coffee. Back in the living room, he sat again in the red chair and put his feet up on the matching ottoman.

Molly and Joseph were already in bed, but when they heard his voice they ran into the living room. Joseph stood in the doorway, smiling quizzically. Molly climbed over Malcolm's legs and onto his lap. Malcolm set the coffee down and Molly burrowed under his arm, into his armpit. He stroked her hair. Marian felt an uneasiness, a tension, and then she was suddenly shaken by yearning—to be held, to be stroked—and she felt dizzy, as if she might faint.

"Now, run along," said Malcolm to the children, "and I'll see you Sunday." As the children left the room, he explained. "They're coming to my new place for lunch on Sunday. If that's all right with you?" She nodded. "Did you know I had a place? It's not exactly elegant, but I like it much better than the hotel. I like having a place of my own."

"This is yours." She slid off her chair and dropped to her knees beside him. She pressed her face against his thigh. He did not move beneath her caresses. When she looked up, she saw the prim set of his lips. She stood up.

"Now, about the arrangements," he said. "Here's what I thought, but I want you to be thoroughly satisfied."

He pulled a folded-up piece of paper from his wallet. It was covered with words and figures in his neat, small handwriting. She saw the words *Insurance* and *Automobile*.

"You really should get a lawyer," he said. She seized upon the kindness in his voice.

"Who should I get?"

He drew one of the black cigarettes from the box. He tamped it against the back of his hand and lighted it with his silver lighter. After a moment, he said, "You've got to start making that kind of decision for yourself, you know."

"Don't you see that it's too late?" she whispered.

He stood up, tapped ashes into the ash tray, drank off the last of the coffee, gathered together his cigarettes and lighter and wallet. "You're a perfectly competent woman," he said, "as no one knows better than I. After all," he went on, smiling at her, his voice remote, jocular, false, "you managed to get me through graduate school. I don't forget that. I'll always be grateful for that."

She went to the window and stared out at the darkness. "Then how can you desert me like this?" Her voice was hoarse, choked.

"There's no point going over this again," he said in an exasperated voice. "I know it's right for both of us."

She heard his sigh, the sound of the ottoman scraping across the floor as he pushed it aside, his footsteps brushing across the rug. The sky was cloudless, starless, moonless. The leaves of the eucalyptus shivered. Dark spaces opened within her. She spoke softly to the windowpane.

"Can't you stay just tonight?"

"Now, Marian," he said, moving into the hallway.

"Just to hold me," she whispered, "in the dark, a last time."

"Good night," he called from the front door. Soon the lights of his car vanished into the dark. She stood at the window a moment longer. She felt the agitation rising, the fury, the rush of movement through her body. She felt the hardness gather in the center of her chest, and she could make no sound.

By early December the ground was soggy with rain. For days the sky was close in and gray. Through the autumn, Marian had become aware of the woman in white, seen as a flash of light out of the corner of her eye as she drove along. The woman was probably a nurse, she thought, cutting through the campus on her way to the university hospital. She was about five-nine or five-ten and very, very thin, like a wraith. She was sway-backed, and as she walked she lifted her knees high, her feet far out in front of her, like a drum majorette on parade. The knobby joints between her long thin bones made her look even more awkward and absurd. Yet she walked without self-consciousness, head high, as if she had better thoughts to ponder than the amusement of people driving by in their big cars. This lack of vanity was one of the characteristics shared by the women who walked. That, and the vigorous, heedless way they moved.

Marian had only seen the wraith—as she came to think of her—in the vicinity of the university until a drizzly Sunday afternoon in early December when she saw her on a downtown street. The children had eaten lunch with Malcolm, and she had contrived to pick them up. Malcolm lived in a cottage behind a large Spanish house close by the freeway. Often she had driven past and stared down the overgrown path that ran alongside the house. Baskets of ferns and wandering Jew hung from the roof of the cottage's dilapidated porch, and there were bright flowered curtains behind the windows. Though appealing in the way that dark, shabby little cottages sometimes are, the charm of this one seemed utterly foreign to everything she believed she knew of Malcolm's taste. He had always insisted that their house be modern and sparse. Something had changed in him, and she thought that if only she could see inside the place she might at last understand what had gone wrong between them. And so she had told him that she was going on an errand and since she didn't want the children to return to an empty house, she would pick them up.

But even before she had turned off the ignition, she saw Molly running down the path toward her and Joseph sauntering behind. Malcolm, in a bright green sweatshirt and jeans, stood on the porch and waved to her as if she were only the mother of children visiting at his house. She was filled with shame at her scheme, with disappointment at its failure, and then with relief.

Joseph got in the front seat. He looked sullen and moody, as he often did after the Sundays with his father. Molly climbed in back and grasped Marian's ears and said, "Giddyap." Marian patted Molly's hands and said, "I'll bet anything you had— let's see—bologna on store-bought bread and Coke. And of course Oreos." The thought of Malcolm's providing such a dreary lunch gave her pleasure, and revving the motor she laughed aloud.

"No," said Joseph. He crossed his arms and dropped his head.

"We had chicken with some kind of orange stuff all over it," said Molly. "I didn't like it, but that lady said I ought to eat it since she made it special."

Joseph turned to the back seat. "Stupid," he hissed. "Nobody can trust you."

Marian thrust her foot against the accelerator, and the car jumped from the curb, bucked, almost died, caught, and sped away. That lady. A woman. No one had told her there was a woman. But who would? Who did she have to tell her anything? Yet she should have known. She was the stupid one. The secrecy. The children's silence. The shabby place with its shabby charm. The ferns. The bright curtains. And behind the curtains, a woman peering out at her, perhaps laughing at her. The rejected wife. The discard. Garbage.

"I didn't mean to tell," said Molly. She patted Marian's shoulder. "I'm sorry."

Marian drove in silence, beneath the immense white oaks,

past the fine old mansions, past the run-down rooming houses
and flats. No life stirred. Even the downtown streets were
empty. The car moved through empty gray streets. The day
was cold, damp, dark. And then she saw a flash of shimmering
white. Without thinking, she said,

"One of the walkers."

The woman strutted toward them on her long heron legs.
She had on a pale pink jacket over her white dress. As the car
drew near, Marian saw that the jacket was short-sleeved, that
it barely covered the woman's breasts, that it was loose-fitting,
flimsy, crocheted. That it was a bed jacket. As Marian stared,
the woman turned toward her. Her eyes were narrowed, glittering, defiant. She grinned fiercely.

"What walkers?" asked Joseph. He dropped his feet from
the dashboard and sat up to see. Marian pressed the accelerator and the car jerked forward, throwing Joseph against
the seat.

"Never mind. We've passed her." Marian flushed with embarrassment. She felt that she had somehow humiliated the
woman in front of Joseph and Molly.

"I saw her," said Molly. "She had on pink and white. Joseph
just doesn't look."

Joseph spun on her. "You shut up, you shut up," he said.
His voice trembled. Marian touched his shoulder.

"Please don't quarrel," she said.

He pulled away from her hand. "I hate you and Daddy!" he
shouted. "You don't care about us, you don't care what you
do to us."

"Mommy didn't do it—did you?" said Molly. "It was Daddy
and that lady."

"He wouldn't have just left," said Joseph. "It was her fault,
too."

Hot moisture bubbled into her eyes, and shrill sounds rose
into her ears. She pulled the car over to the curb. Now she
would tell them. Her fault? Her fault, too? Now she would
unleash her suffering, she would engulf them in her anguish.
She would tell them, she would tell them. She turned to

Joseph. His eyelids were slightly lowered, and his nose and mouth were stretched down and pinched. She twisted to see Molly.

"Don't," said Molly. "Please don't look like thât. Don't cry. Please don't cry. You're so ugly when you cry. Please don't."

Marian pressed her fingers into her skull. She held her neck muscles taut. She pushed out her chest and belly to make room for the expanding pressure. They were her children. They were all she had now. She must protect them from misery and pain. From herself. In the rearview mirror, she could make out in the gray distance the comic cakewalk of the woman in white, alone, in the cold.

Over the next weeks, she longed to tell Malcolm that she knew about the woman. She longed to taunt him. How typical, how trite, how sordid. He had deserted his family for the sleaziest of reasons, another woman, a younger woman, probably a graduate student. Malcolm with his dignity and pride. How comical it was. She saw herself pick up the telephone and dial his number. She heard her contemptuous yet amused voice ringing through the wires. Sleazy and comical, she heard herself say.

But she did not call him. She was afraid. His voice would be hard and irritable, and he would say hateful things to her that she could not bear to hear. She imagined his saying, I never loved you, not even at the beginning. She heard him say, I married you only so I could finish my degree. He would infect her memories with doubt and ruin the past for her. He would leave her with nothing. While he had the woman.

Through the winter months, she spent hours at a time daydreaming about Malcolm and his woman. Often, she sat at her bedroom window and watched the rain break against the pane. She believed that if she concentrated hard enough, she would be able to conjure up an image of the woman. But always as the face began to form on the film of the glass, the wind swept the image away.

One day as the outline of the eyes appeared, she leaned

close to fasten the face to the windowpane. She saw her own reflection, and she saw that her eyes were more haggard than she remembered, her lips thin, her nose taut. She had grown suddenly old and ugly. She drew back from the windowpane, and as she did, her reflection began to move away from her, as if the image were running to a distant point in the street. She saw her reflection grow smaller and smaller, and then vanish.

She jumped from the chair and rushed into the living room. She must come out of her misery. She had lost touch with the world, gone stale and sour inside herself. Her life had lost its shape. She had no purpose. She had been only marking time, waiting for relief that would never come. She had to build her life again, become a person again.

She sat down in the red chair, Malcolm's chair. No, she thought, it's my chair. She pulled the *New York Times Magazine* from the mahogany rack by the chair. The magazine was six months old. She dumped all the magazines on the floor, the *New Republic, Harper's*, the *New York Review of Books*. They were all stiff and yellow with age. Malcolm's magazines. He had taken the subscriptions with him, and she had not even missed them. She had read nothing in months.

The blood rose to her head and pounded behind her eyes. She had once been an attractive, interesting woman who kept up, who could talk of anything. Yes, talk so that men listened to her and admired her and desired her. Malcolm had taken all that from her. That, too. Slowly, slowly. Over the years. He had frequently said hurtful things to her—that she had chattered, that she had told a story in boring detail. Hurtful things that had made her feel inadequate or silly and that broke her confidence. She had given up, content to let him do the talking, content with the warmth of his brilliance. To please him, she became a cipher. And when he thought he had completed her destruction, he had deserted her.

But he was wrong—she was not destroyed. Free of him, she was ready to become the attractive woman she had once been. Everything was still there, ready to emerge from the half-life she had lived all these years. She felt that her powers

26

were flooding back to her, washing away her fear of him and her timidity.

Exultant, triumphant, she rushed to the telephone and dialed his number at the university. But when a soft young female voice answered, she could not speak. She heard Malcolm say, "Who is it, Teddy?" and then "Hello," into the phone. She could not remember what she had intended to say to him. A pressure began, swelled larger and larger until she feared it would explode in her chest, crash through her eardrums, shatter the delicate membranes of her nostrils and eyes. She opened her mouth to let the sounds out, but no sound came.

Marian had often noticed the woman in the red plastic coat who walked with one hand palm-up at her shoulder and the other on her hip. Her white hair was burnished to a metallic sheen, and it stood high above her face, like a chef's cap. She wore multicolored platform shoes with six-inch heels that threw her forward, and she took quick little mincing steps as if hurrying to catch up with her body before it fell. She was, Marian decided, probably a prostitute.

But prostitute or not, she was a human being and a woman, and a woman obviously mistreated by men. And so seeing her on a drizzly March afternoon walking with the red coat held straight-armed above her elaborate hairdo, Marian decided to give the woman a lift. She drew the car alongside the curb and leaned across the passenger seat to lower the window.

And then she noticed the sores on the woman's bare legs. Some of the sores were black holes with diameters the size of a pencil, some were raw-looking with moist crusts, and some were fresh, suppurating, leaving faint trails down her calves. The woman turned. Her face was mottled and skull-like, and the flesh seemed already to be rotting back from the bones.

Marian felt a hard spasm in her lower belly, as if a steel hand had fastened around her groin. The woman grinned then, a terrible grin of complicity, as if she had anticipated, had desired, now shared, the sudden hatred Marian felt surging through

27

her. As Marian reared back from the window and twisted the steering wheel toward the street, she heard a muffled, constricted whimpering, and she knew it was her own.

One Sunday afternoon in June, Malcolm came into the house with the children. It had been nearly a year since he had left; the divorce was final. He stood in the hallway and leaned casually against the wall. He was deeply tanned, and his gray sideburns were long and bushy and somehow boyish. He seemed cheerful and lighthearted, qualities she thought he had long ago given up to his seriousness, his image of himself as a scholar. He wore his new happiness like an advertisement, and his smile seemed to suggest that she rejoice with him.

He said, "I've got a plan I know you're going to like."

Her resentment was like a coagulant. As he spoke, her blood and her energy ceased to flow, and she felt sullen, dull, thick.

He told her that he would take the children for July to one of the San Juan Islands off Seattle. No electricity, he exulted. No cars. No telephone. Just man against nature, with the necessities flown in, he said, laughing archly. He had never been there, of course, but—he paused no more than a heartbeat—he knew someone who had. He began to describe the island, as if he were enticing her to come along, the cliffs, the immense trees, the wild berries, the birds.

"This will be one of the best experiences of their lives," he said, "and you'll be free for a whole month."

"Free to do what?" she asked. Her tongue was thick and heavy, and her voice hardly rose to her mouth.

"See you next Sunday," he called to the children, and waving, waving, he backed out the front door.

"I'm going to have a shell collection," Molly said.

"There's a lot of driftwood," said Joseph, "so you can carve things and all."

"I'm going to make you a beautiful shell necklace. Teddy says the shells are beautiful."

"Be quiet," said Joseph.

"I've never been to an island," Molly went on. "I wish you could come, too."

"Yeah," said Joseph.

After her hot bath, she lay in bed in the dark, staring at the odd shapes the moon cast against the draperies. The moon on the water and the sandy beaches and the shadows of trees. The wind blew in her open window and the draperies billowed. She saw people in the moving folds. Heads. Bodies. Lovers moving against each other in the dark shadows. Malcolm and his woman. She drew her hands along her hips, squeezed her breasts between her fingers. No one would ever hold her, whisper to her in the night. For a moment she feared that she would scream out in her anguish, and she threw back the covers and sat up on the side of the bed.

If only she had someone to talk to, to whom she could tell her suffering. She thought of her parents, both dead, and of the brother she had not seen in years. The faces of girls she had been close to came to her, and one in particular who had blond hair in a Dutch-boy cut and who had moved away when they were both eleven. She thought of a boy whose name she could not recall who had given her chocolates in a heart-shaped box and had kissed her clumsily on the ear. And of the boy who had loved her in high school and whom she had loved until she had met Malcolm. All these, and others she might have talked to, were gone.

When she got up to close the window against the wind, she saw a light beneath Joseph's door. Molly had already deserted her—she had said "Teddy" in an affectionate, accepting way. But Joseph, her first-born, suffered as she did.

She went to his room. He lay prone on his bed, propped on his elbows, a book open in front of him. She said, "I want to talk to you."

He folded the book over his finger and turned over. He lay back against the headboard. The light from the bullet lamp fell across the side of his face. He looked frail and sad.

29

She sat down in the desk chair and dragged it closer to the bed. "You're going away," she said, "with them." She held his gaze.

"Mom, please don't," he said. His shadowed face turned away from her. "We're not supposed to talk about the other one. He nevers talks about you."

"Never? Has he never said anything?"

"All he ever said was, he had a right to try to be happy," Joseph said in a soft, fretful, placating voice. He drew his knees up and folded his arms across them and buried his head in his arms. "Please don't talk to me, please," he said.

As he lifted his face to her, his head seemed to rise above his knees, disembodied. As she stared at him, his face grew larger and larger and whiter and whiter. It swelled toward her, a pale disc, like the moon. She got to her feet.

"Sleep well," she said.

She went into the kitchen to make sure she had turned off the oven and the burners. She checked the locks on outside doors. She listened for the sound of a forgotten sprinkler. The house was still and dark and hot. She felt dull and sluggish, yet she was excited, too restless to stay inside.

She went into her bathroom and took her old flannel robe off the hook on the back of the door. She got in the car and drove over to the university lake. In the springtime, the students boated and swam and sunned at the lake, and often she and Malcolm had brought the children there to search for tadpoles and frogs. Now, in June, the lake was slowly drying into a swamp.

She sat on the dark bank and breathed in the cool night air. The moon shimmered in the puddles on the lake bottom. It was the end of the spring term, and she heard the murmur of student lovers and the rustle of dry leaves. She imagined bodies touching, and the soft delicious look of desire on their mouths and in their eyes. She had known that ecstasy. She remembered the first night she and Malcolm had been together. They had been on Cape Cod. She saw them lying in a little pocket of leafy brush, protected from the wind by an overhanging cliff. She had felt nothing existed but the two of them, and nothing mattered but the act of love they performed.

And in the moonlight, sitting on the damp bank of the swampy lake, she began to cry. Her crying was a moan that returned to her as the sound of soft thunder. And then she saw movement in the shadows of the trees. The students, the lovers, were moving away. In her groin was the pain that was like lust, like fear, like hatred. She didn't care what the lovers or anyone thought of her. Her chest swelled with sobs. They seemed to be exploding in her ribs, bursting from her armpits, ripping through her ears and eye sockets.

She stood up. The streets were empty. She clutched her bathrobe tighter against the suddenly chilly night, and she began to walk quickly, recklessly, in the direction of the moon. As she walked, she felt the power of her thrusting stride, the rising flood of her energy, the release of her torment.

The Day the Tree Fell Down

They had gone to a party, they had drunk a little too much, they slept restlessly. During the early morning hours, an autumn storm roared into their little suburban valley. Wind whipped the branches of the trees against the walls of the house. Rain crashed on the windows. Wires twanged eerily.

Dozing fitfully, they thought of Sunday pleasures ahead. Carrie decided she would start the new Stegner. She would listen to the whole of *Don Giovanni*. Frederick wondered if the rain would stop in time for his Sunday afternoon tennis game. The 49ers were in L.A.—that'd be a good game. And he had the Kissinger, too.

At six o'clock, the furnace came on. The bed grew hot and where they touched, they sweated.

"You forgot to change the timer to the Sunday setting," Carrie muttered.

"You forgot," Frederick muttered. They moved apart. Frederick thought maybe he wouldn't mend the jalousie after all. Carrie thought maybe she wouldn't fix the pot roast with anchovies the way he liked it.

Soon, sounds from the rest of the house came to them. Their son Jack thumped a basketball against the garage. How many times had he been told it would smudge the paint, Carrie wondered. Their daughter Emily opened and closed kitchen cabinets. Frederick hoped she wasn't standing on one of the rickety chairs. You'd think kids could wait until a decent hour.

Jack rushed into the room just before ten o'clock. "You've slept enough," he shouted. "You've got to come outside." After him came Emily, almost gleaming.

"I can't," said Carrie. "I'd get arrested. I'm naked."

Jack laughed. Emily said, "You could get dressed and then come."

"What's so all-fired important?" Frederick asked.

"You'll never guess," said Jack. "How much you want to bet?"

"Bad odds," said Frederick. He pulled the covers over his head.

"Come see," said Jack. "Please."

"Please," said Emily.

And so of course they got up. The sun was shining—it was going to be a nice day. Frederick put on tennis whites. Carrie put on jeans. They splashed water on their faces, brushed their teeth, went outside.

Their tree. Their lovely zelkova.

The tree lay sprawled across the driveway, felled by the storm. Its trunk was broken as clean as if it had been no more than a matchstick. Its low branches had just missed the front of the garage, its high branches blocked the driveway. Leaves, brittle with autumn, were scattered across the walk and into the street.

"How about that?" said Jack. "Worth getting up for?"

Carrie felt a loss, an ache. The only real specimen tree they had. Elegant. Guests walking up the drive saw it, admired it. Gone. And with it the three hundred and fifty dollars Frederick had so reluctantly paid. She waited to hear his thunder.

Gone just like that, Frederick thought. It must have been a helluva storm to snap a trunk ten inches thick. Or a weak tree. They should have bought the Chinese elm as she had wanted. But he had fallen for the zelkovas. And now this—an ugly scar on her landscaping, after she had worked so hard. He waited to feel her lightning.

"I'm going to tell about it tomorrow in Show and Tell," said Emily.

Jack whirled on her. "You can't. I'm the one that found it."

"I would have," she answered. "You don't own it, it belongs to the whole family."

33

"You wouldn't have found it for hours," Jack said. "You never go outside until your friends call you."

"That's not so," said Emily. "I'm outside now."

"Cut it out," said Frederick. "Quarreling just makes it worse."

"Emily can tell it in her class," said Carrie, "and Jack can tell it in his. Okay?"

"It'll be a sad story," said Emily. She leaned over and touched the pale yellow pulp where the trunk had snapped. "Poor old tree. It's sure dead."

"You probably thought trees lived forever," said Jack. "Everything dies. You're alive and then bang! you're dead."

"I know that," said Emily, standing up. "And when you die they either burn you up or put you in a hole in the ground and throw dirt over you." Carrie took Emily's head in the crook of her elbow and kissed her hair.

"Such serious thoughts," Carrie said. "It's just a tree."

"We're going to burn it up," said Jack. "In the fireplace."

Frederick lifted a dangling branch and let it fall. It was blocking the drive—he'd have to do something. It would take hours to get the limbs off, more hours to saw them into logs. "I wish it hadn't happened on Sunday," he said. He quickly twisted his eyeballs to see Carrie. He hoped she hadn't heard him.

She had. She said, "Any other day and I'd have to handle the whole thing by myself. Right?"

Frederick was sure he had been joking. He laughed. "Hey, Jack, let's pretend it hasn't happened. Let's you not discover it until tomorrow morning when I've got eight minutes to run to the train." He put his hand on Carrie's neck and shook her playfully. She jerked away.

"You'd do it, too," she said. "If you thought you could get away with it."

"God," answered Frederick, "where'd you park your sense of humor this morning?"

Just then they heard a loud whistle. Their two-doors-down neighbor stood at the front of his drive, stooped in wonderment. "Freddie baby," he yelled, "you sure get your firewood the hard way." Frederick smiled sourly.

Soon the whole neighborhood gathered to see the fallen tree. Everyone commiserated, offered advice, and grinned. Carrie wondered what was funny about losing a perfectly beautiful and expensive tree. Frederick had an idea.

"Who's for a tree-dismantling party?" he asked. "All the beer you can drink? We'll get in some sandwiches?"

Really they wanted to, they said, but there was church, there was a promise to take the kids somewhere, there was company coming. They'd sure try to get back. They left, hiding their grins.

"Neighbors," said Frederick bitterly. "You'd think they'd be willing to lend a hand."

"It's our tree, our problem," said Carrie. "Let's get to work."

Frederick hunkered down and tore off a twig. He put the bare end in his mouth. It was bitter and he spat it out. "We should have bought that small tree, the way I wanted. One, it wouldn't have snapped in two. Two, if it had it still wouldn't be so much work to get rid of it."

Carrie felt her heart skip. She stuck her fists in the pockets of her jeans. "As I said at the time," she said, "the Chinese elm would have been much better. But you would have a zelkova. Though you'd never seen one before." She felt a little trembling in her stomach—anger gathering. He felt a pressure on his back teeth. Damn good thing he had gold crowns.

"Come on, you guys, don't stand there blabbing," said Jack. "We have work to do."

Frederick stood up. "Look: I have a rusty saw with half its teeth broken off, an ax with a handle held together with Elmer's glue, and a hatchet Jack used to break up that concrete block. Is there really an inherent virtue in me spending the whole day trying to skin this tree? The tree man's going to have to take out the trunk and roots anyway. I mean, unless you expect me to do that, too."

"I'll help," said Emily.

He dropped his hand to her shoulder. "Yeah, well, even with good help. Sunday? My one day?" He felt outraged. Surely he had a right to one day. He worked hard five and a

35

half days a week, fiddling with other people's accounts, other people's tax problems. And Saturday afternoons he took Emily and Jack for an outing so that Carrie could do whatever. Not that he minded—he liked those outings. But even God rested on the seventh day. "Anyway, I was planning to put a new handle on the jalousie."

"That should take four and a quarter minutes," Carrie said. She knew he wasn't thinking about the jalousie. He could have done that months ago, when she had first asked him. He acted as if it were a personal favor to her, as if he didn't even live there. "Maybe just one Sunday you don't absolutely have to play tennis with your pals."

"You're absolutely right," he answered, nodding vigorously. "I don't absolutely have to play tennis with my pals. A fact. But," he lifted his index finger to make the point, "I want to. That, too, is a fact. And anyway, what's it to you, so long as we get somebody to do it?"

"What's it to me?" she repeated. "What's it to me?" And then it was miraculously before her. "Who's going to call that famous tree man and set up the appointment? Who'll have to stick home for five days waiting for him to show up? Who'll have to stand around making sure nobody drops a limb on the azaleas? Who'll sweep up the mess when they're finished? Raise your hand if you know the answer to that one." Laughing, the children raised their hands.

Frederick flushed and glared at the tree. Why she thought he had intended to saddle her with the trouble was beyond him. Or had he? Actually, he didn't mind missing the football game—mostly he just read the Sunday paper and only looked at the screen when the announcer's voice got excited or there was a replay. But he'd be damned if he'd give up his one time to exercise for the week. He was going to play tennis, tree or no tree. It was already late October—the cold would be upon them soon.

"And by the way," she said before he could speak, "I figure to skin the branches and cut them into logs will add about one hundred dollars to this little job." She could think of better ways to spend the money. Well, she'd like a subscription to the Wednesday afternoon concert series in the city. She missed music—it had been a large part of her life for years. Just because he was tone deaf . . . And maybe hit the museum in the morning, see some shows she only read about. She hadn't been to the city alone in four months. Twice she had met Frederick for dinner; once she took the kids to the science museum. "A hundred bucks for a tennis game?" She almost snorted. Of course he got to go to the city all the time.

He wouldn't even look at her, he was so angry. What an unfair way to put it. A hundred-dollar tennis game. And anyway he hadn't said definitely that he wouldn't do the job. He looked at his watch. The tennis game was set for two o'clock. He could probably finish the work by then, if he had a little help. He'd saw the big limbs; Jack could use the hatchet to strip off the little ones; Carrie could take care of the debris, get everything off to the side; and Emily . . . well, he'd find something for her to do. Then maybe next week he'd saw the limbs into proper lengths for the fireplace. Rugged work.

"I guess this job won't take that long," he said.

"At the rate you're going, it could be spring," said Carrie.

Again, Jack and Emily laughed. Frederick's jawline clamped down and his eyebrows folded together. Immediately she was sorry she'd spoken. God, she just couldn't resist the standing target. She reached across the trunk of the tree to touch his hard jaw, but he snapped his head out of her reach. She said, "Look, don't do it, don't bother. I was making a fuss over nothing. Okay?" But he wasn't having any.

"Who'll call that famous tree man and who'll guard the azaleas and . . . no, thanks," he said. "The price, though not the money, is far too high. You'll make me pay for months."

"What can I do to help?" she asked.

"Not a thing. I'd rather you didn't." He walked off to the garage. He got the saw, the hatchet, the ax. When he came back, Carrie was gone. See? Now who had squirmed out of the work?

She had taken a last sorrowful look at the broken tree and the wounded landscape, and gone inside. They would have quarreled if she had stayed to help. He would have ended up whacking off his toes. Or hers. Better to stay out of Vesuvius' way when he was blowing. Later, he would come in in triumph, the goal achieved, looking deliciously smug. Nice.

She went to the record cabinet and took out *Don Giovanni*, replaced it, took out Moussorgsky's *Pictures at an Exhibition*. Frederick had often said that was his favorite music after . . . what was it? Ravel's *Bolero*? Funny man. She turned up the volume as loud as it would go and pulled the speakers toward the window. She raised the window. Behind her, violins soared, horns blared. Thinking it would amuse him, she conducted the music with great swooping gestures. The music, the crowds, the musicians with intent faces responding to her least gesture. Funny, despite her years of violin, it had never occurred to her to become a conductor. Playing in the college orchestra was about her limit. And she had become a trainee at the bank. She called for the tympani.

Frederick stood straight up. His hand with the saw dropped to his side. His other hand came up to his hip. Carrie closed the window, lowered the volume. Okay, if he wanted to stay mad, let him. She sat on the ottoman and hummed along with the music. Of course it was foolish to think about becoming a conductor. It was too late and she probably wouldn't be good enough anyway. She remembered the beds to be made, lunch to be fixed, a letter she ought to write her mother. She turned off the record player.

Why she thought he would want to listen to that music while he sawed was beyond him. The rhythm going about twice as fast as he could, sawing, and those horns honking in his brain. He didn't mind if she listened, of course—probably did that half the day while he was at work. No wonder she had a better ear than he did. He couldn't recognize anything but Beethoven's Fifth and the Moussorgsky thing. She knew them all, Mozart, Bartok, all those birds. And all the writers and painters who had ever lived. By God, he'd sure like that, his life one long college education, sitting around reading, listening to whosever music that was, instead of spending what little spare time he had sawing on a dead tree. A lot of men wouldn't even be home on a Sunday. Fishing, drinking, women. Sailing was what he had liked—his little catamaran, pulling hard against the wind, the sun glinting on the water, and, in the old days, a pretty girl with her tan legs sprawled out, her shirt flapping, her hair streaming behind her. God, you'd think the damn tree was made of iron, it was so hard to saw.

After two hours he had only taken off the biggest limbs on one side. The poor tree looked as if some giant had been gnawing on it. He didn't have the proper tools and the kids weren't any help. A friend of Jack's had come over and the two boys had been constantly at war, using small branches to anni-hilate each other through the eyeballs. When Frederick had told them to stop, the friend had just quit and then Jack had been tight-lipped for a while. And Frederick never knew where Emily was, but pretty soon her little hand would dart under the limb he was working on. Twice he almost nicked her finger. You'd think Carrie could at least have found some-thing inside for Emily to do.

"For Pete's sake, Emily," he said, "don't be hovering right where I'm trying to saw. Look, why don't you go ask your mother if she's going to deign to fix lunch today."

Instantly Emily was in tears and running up the driveway to the house and he was calling after her, "Emily, come back, please, Emily. I need your help." She disappeared inside.

He certainly hadn't meant that the way she had taken it. Ac-tually, he was glad to have her help—at least one female will-ing to do something besides sit on her can all day. But she was probably pouring it all out to Carrie right that minute.

"Come on, Dad," Jack said in a querulous voice. "At this rate we'll be here all day."

"Just quit," Frederick said furiously. "Everybody just quit and leave it all to me."

Jack looked at the ground. "I just meant I want to finish be-cause we're having a football game this afternoon."

Frederick remembered his tennis game. He glanced at his watch. It was nearly one o'clock already. "Okay," he said, "let's break for lunch and start up again about four."

"That's when the football is," said Jack.

"Well, if your football game is so all-fired important . . ." He stopped, looked at the tree, the house, the top of Jack's head. "You have a right to your Sunday game," he said. He leaned the saw against the trunk of the tree. He was pretty close to done. A few more big limbs off and he'd be able to drag the tree from the driveway so Carrie could get her car out. There wasn't much point in sawing it up for firewood. It would take a year to dry. Have to stack the logs against the back of the house. Another Sunday gone. The danger of termites. Fire, even, maybe. Let the trash man haul the damn thing off.

In the kitchen, Emily was sitting on Carrie's lap and when she saw Frederick she buried her head in Carrie's shoulder. Frederick drew up a chair.

"Look, Em," he said, patting her knee. "I'm sorry I hurt your feelings. I just didn't want you to get hurt is all. I appreciate your help." He shook her ankle playfully. "Forgiven?" Emily looked at him and nodded grudgingly.

Carrie thought Frederick looked sad. And very tense. She'd suggest that he go and play tennis. That would relax him. Tomorrow she would talk the trash man into hauling the tree away. Give him twenty dollars.

"You didn't have any breakfast," she said. "You're probably dying of hunger." She lifted Emily into his lap and walked to the stove.

"I could eat," he said. Carrie, ladling soup into bowls, smiled at him. He began to feel a lot better. "I hope it's quick. I don't want to be late for my tennis game."

Carrie stopped ladling. She felt tricked, betrayed. He hadn't canceled? "Then you've finished and I can get the car out."

The decision was before him: which way would he jump? He decided not to get angry again. He nuzzled Emily. "Your mother thinks I don't do enough around here. But who looks for burglars in the middle of the night? Who got the bird out of the living room draperies last summer? And who took Fritzy to the vet when he got his ear bitten off? I ask you, who?"

40

"You," said Emily, nuzzling back. "You do a lot."

"Anyway, you make the money," said Jack.

"A rather indispensable and handsome contribution to the household, if I do say so myself." He looked at Carrie. Her back was not smiling.

Resentment burst through her. His money. Because he was a man—the provider. Her eyes felt dry, scalded. Her heart beat into her throat. As though she were some kind of inferior being, a child, a chattel. She had been going places at the bank, long before anybody's Affirmative Anything. But then they had married and right away the babies—of course she was glad about the babies, it wasn't their fault. But still. Women with half her ability were vice-presidents already, running branches. Her college roommate went to conferences in Brussels and Copenhagen. While she went to the meat market and the Childrens' Boots. And then he threw the money up to her. Smug. Arrogant. Well, she was only thirty-four, her brain hadn't totally disintegrated yet. Not yet. The children practically took care of themselves. They didn't really need her anymore. Plenty of women these days were canceling marriages that had gone sour, that didn't fit anymore. On their own, came and went as they pleased, answered to nobody. Not taking that "my money" off anyone.

"Haven't we said thanks often enough this week?" She curled an angry look from under her eyelids. She put the bowl in front of him. A little of the hot soup sloshed out, and he jerked his hands off the table. She walked out of the room.

"I don't think she liked that," said Jack.

"I'm still going to go!" Frederick shouted at her retreating back.

He was furious. She put the worst construction on everything he said. He couldn't even joke. Deliberately distorted. He had never once thrown money at her. Joint account. Joint decisions right down the line. But he did go out of the house every damn morning at 7:15 and went to work and worked hard, and it was not exactly peaches and cream either. And then for her to imply he expected to be thanked—that was rotten. Tyranny. Psychological tyranny because he was a nice guy and she could get away with it. Well, twelve years was quite long enough, thank you. No more. He had managed twenty-six years without her, and damn well, too. And now he knew how to enjoy it. God, there was so much he hadn't seen, hadn't done. Exotic places. Beautiful women on the street. He noticed but never answered the looks he got. God, he never even stopped at a bar on the way home to talk to his friends. For what? For nasty looks and a vicious temper. Twelve whole years.

She went into the bedroom and put on her windbreaker. She would do the tree herself. Through the bedroom window, she saw his bicycle disappear around the corner, and she felt wild inside. So—he really went.

When she went back into the kitchen, Jack and Emily were putting their soup bowls into the dishwasher. When she asked if they were going to help her finish the tree, they said they were tired, and anyway they had already done their share. Rage pressed against her chest and tears flashed across her eyes. Left with the mess. As usual. Okay. Okay. She would do it alone. She didn't need him. Them. Anybody. She was her own person, answered to nobody. Thank God. At last.

She went outside to the tree. It looked as though its limbs had been twisted off instead of sawed. It had once been beautiful, majestic, but now after his clumsy efforts it was ugly.

She couldn't keep the saw steady. She had to make a dozen cuts before she found the groove. Then she sawed. And sawed. He didn't keep his saw in very good condition. No bite. Rusty. Her father's tools were always shiny and sharp. Her father had been a patriarch. Domineering. At least he never left messes for someone else to finish and clean up.

Finally the limb fell. She started another. Her shoulder began to ache and she thought she was getting a blister on the heel of her hand. She shifted the saw to her left hand. The saw jumped out of the groove. She decided she would finish that branch later. She ripped off two small branches and put them on Emily's pile. The street was empty. Everybody was enjoying Sunday. She felt the sweat rolling down her sides, and yet she was cold. The sun had vanished behind an overlay of gray clouds. It had become a cold wintry afternoon, darkening, somber.

Frederick's tennis was terrible. He totally missed one easy overhead and double-faulted set point in the first set. She never appreciated a damn thing he did. Like when he gave up his vacation time to take care of the kids while she went to her brother's wedding. A whole week cooking, even trying to iron, while she was living it up in Lake Forrest. And when she came back, she just instinctively made for the shirt he had scorched. And laughed and said Now you know how the other half lives. As though he didn't, as though he was some insensitive Neanderthal. He poached a shot and sent the ball ricocheting off the back fence.

At first Frederick's friends ragged him. Lost the good eye? Gone soft in your old age? How could he play tennis when his stomach was a hard rock and the blood was pounding behind his eyeballs? Give her credit—she had power, she ruined everything. Why did he tolerate it? It probably wasn't even good for the kids.

In the middle of the second set, he touched his brow. "I think I must be coming down with something."

"I think so, too," said his tight-lipped partner.

"If you guys don't mind . . . ?" Frederick asked.

Carrie remembered the pot roast. Once she got that going, she'd finish the tree. She put down the saw and went into the kitchen. She had to laugh—sawing off the top of a carrot was a whole lot easier than sawing off the limb of a tree. Perhaps Frederick was right and they should get a tree man in. A tree man with his power saws and pulleys and that machine that ate up leaves and twigs. They should just buy their firewood.

She walked into the living room and put on *Don Giovanni*. The afternoon was almost gone. A terrible day. It could have been so nice. Reading in the twin armchairs. Music. And then in late afternoon a fire in the fireplace. That tree. It had somehow fallen down between them. She turned the volume up a little. The music swelled around her. She remembered how she used to be able to lose herself in music. Slowly her shoulders began to relax down off her ears. The tension flowed away along her arms. Her belly softened. She was always throwing up impossible goals, demanding that Frederick do it her way or else. She would just close her eyes and listen, for a few minutes. And then she would go back to that poor old tree.

Frederick parked his bicycle against the garage. He'd just finish the damn tree. He began to saw. The work seemed to go more quickly without the children there. It was a good feeling, really, to do something physical and useful. Maybe during the week he would have the saw and the ax cleaned and sharpened, and next Sunday he would hew the trunk and the big limbs into logs for the fireplace. God, there'd be enough to last years. Sitting beside a good fire. Sunday afternoons in the rainy season and chilly evenings.

It was dusk when Carrie awoke. The house was silent and dark. Frederick had been gone an awfully long time. In the old days when Jack was a baby, Frederick would sometimes play tennis for two or three hours and then go drink beer another couple of hours. Off covorting with his friends while she kept company with a sleeping baby. When he realized how lonely and blue it made her feel, he began to come home right after the game. So dear and thoughtful. It had made her feel a little guilty—he worked hard all week and naturally he wanted to spend some time with his friends. But he said he'd really rather be with her. Not that she wanted him there if he didn't want to be there. After the first year or two, it hadn't been all that exciting. Marriage. All the edges worn smooth. But then you'd find an occasional rough spot.

As Frederick worked his way up the tree, his back began to ache and he was sure he would never be able to straighten his fingers holding the saw. He was just plain tired. He sat down on the trunk of the tree with the saw across his knees and his fists on his thighs. The sky was low and yellow-black in the dusk. You got glimmers of Indian summer and then the cold clamped down. Darkness coming faster every day. He would never finish the tree today. He might as well have gone on with the tennis. His friends hadn't been very nice about his quitting. Long suspicious glances. Not that they were friends. They were tennis pals. He had work pals, he had tennis pals, he and Carrie had couple pals. He didn't have what you could call a real friend like in the old days. Carrie was the only one he ever really talked to. Marriage did that, built a wall.

"Jack?" she called. "Emily?" She was alone in the house. Pretty soon, Jack would come home covered with mud and bruises, recounting tales of triumph and tragedy in his world, and soon Emily would probably telephone to ask if she could go for pizza with her friend's family. They were growing up. Before she knew it, they would be gone and she and Frederick would be alone. Where was Frederick anyway? It wasn't like him to be vengeful and unforgiving. She went from room to room, pausing to look through each doorway, hoping to find him waiting for her in the dark. She opened the door and stepped out into the cold.

He picked at the bark of tree and broke off a section. A tree. A trivial matter, no doubt, but it had made him sad all day. You planted it, watered it, fertilized it, pruned it. It had sap, seeds, leaves, sometimes a flight of birds or a colony of caterpillars. And then one morning it was dead. Logs. Firewood. Ashes. He felt lousy, with the sweat drying on him in the wind and his whole body aching. Was he coming down with something after all? He touched his face with his fingertips. Warmish. He would ask Carrie to feel his forehead. Her cool palm on his brow, brushing back his damp hair. She handed him a hot toddy. She connected the heating pad and placed it beside him in the bed. Then he saw the shadow moving across the light from the house, toward him. Was she still angry? He didn't think he could stand it if she were.

She sat down on the trunk of the tree, a foot or so from him. She looked down at the point where the tree had broken. In the dusk, the wound was a pale greenish white and the wood looked soft, almost fleshy. It was up to her to speak—she knew that. It was hard to speak. Sometimes she found it easier

45

to keep on being mad. But how lonely that made her feel, and almost afraid.

"You've done a lot," she said. "We can pull it out of the way now and get someone in tomorrow to haul the whole thing off."

He looked at her and she was looking at him.

"After all that work?" he said. "We're going to burn up every last splinter. It'll keep us warm for years." He smiled. She held out her hand and he took it and together they looked at the tree.

Jellyfish

The cottage was on a bluff overlooking the beach. It was made of weathered cedar planks trimmed in shiny royal blue. The yard was covered with crushed seashells, with here and there a piece of driftwood, a large blue pot of succulents, a bed of marigolds. There was a vine-covered fence, and under an arbor of climbing pink roses was a little blue gate held by a rough rope latch. Below the bluff, the morning sun glittered on the dark green water of the quiet bay and the water sucked softly at the shore.

"Goddammit," said Elizabeth. "All this clean air, all these bright blue skies. What an exile."

She stood at the door of the screen porch, her head thrust forward, her fingers like claws on her hipbones. That was the mood she was in. Sarah and Preston sat in wicker chairs, staring at the straw rug. Nothing had happened yet—it was all talk. But they were frightened. When she was like this, anything could set her off worse. Sarah thought that if she pinched the inside of her thigh until it hurt, then maybe Elizabeth would stop being so angry. But she didn't like to do it if it wasn't necessary.

"Aw, Mom, you said you'd try," Preston said in a whiney voice.

Sarah said, "I like it here. It's more fun than the city."

Elizabeth glanced over her shoulder at them and twisted her lips. "My pals," she said, "my sympathetic pals."

"It's the last chance," said Preston.

Elizabeth wheeled on him. "Oh, it is, is it? Is that your final word?"

Preston ducked his head and looked at the floor. "That's what he said."

"And what he says is called The Law," said Elizabeth, "and what he is is the Great Lawgiver and what I am is the Lawless One and what you are . . ."

"Please, Mom," said Sarah. She dug her nails into her thigh. It was hard to make herself do it until it really hurt, but she thought she did this time.

Elizabeth put her hand against the door jamb and leaned her head on her hand. They could see the sigh shake through her body and her shoulders drop. When she turned to face them, she was smiling—the mood had vanished. The pinch had worked.

"Innocent victims of the shoot-out, I guess," she said. She pulled Sarah from her seat and held her for a moment and held Preston's head in the crook of her elbow. "Haven't I been absolutely marvelous for three whole weeks? Tell me in all honesty, have I or haven't I been marvelous? Even with the Great Lawgiver himself coming down every weekend to snoop in every cabinet."

Carrying their fishing poles and a cup of bait, they walked down the gravel road to the cove. Along the way, they stopped and listened at the cottages of their summertime friends. No one was about yet.

They went out on the dock. Sarah hated putting worms on the hooks, and she hated asking Preston to do it for her. He always sighed and said if she was too young to bait the hook, she was too young to fish. She didn't like to fish anyway. She just liked being there. She leaned the fishing pole against the railing and sat on the platform with her bare feet dangling over the water.

The water was clear and still in the cove and she looked at the pretty-colored stones on the bottom. Occasionally a fish swished past. Off to the side, near a pile of large dark rocks, the water shimmered in the sunlight. A pinkish mass floated between the surface of the water and the rocks. She remembered that the summer before she had seen a jellyfish in the water. She had reached down to touch it and it had stung her. She felt sick all day. She sighed. No swimming today.

"Do you think she will?" she asked Preston.

She knew he heard her because he began to chew on the back of his tongue. But when he didn't answer, she said again, "Do you think she will?"

"Will what? Who will what?" It was like a threat, as though he wanted to hurt her. "Go on. You started it. Now finish it. Will what?"

If she finished it, he would feel bad too. "Be with those people, that man at the boardwalk, and get drunk."

Preston stopped biting his tongue. "I don't know and I don't care," he said in a low voice. "It's their funeral. Except it's really her funeral."

"Isn't it his funeral, too?" asked Sarah.

"No. He'll get us. He knows how to do it."

He knew how to do almost everything, Sarah thought. He could read in a foreign language and he could play chess and he could throw the football almost all the way down the block for Preston to run and catch. And yet he seemed so tired and sad all the time. And sometimes he didn't speak to their mother for days and not very much to Sarah and Preston, though he never got angry with them the way their mother did. Even at dinner he wouldn't talk. Elizabeth would stare at him, looking sad too, and then say something funny to Sarah or Preston, like "Run upstairs and get my down jacket, I'm beginning to feel the chill" or "I didn't quite catch that, would you repeat it, please." Sarah's father often would drop his napkin in the middle of his plate and leave the table and lock himself in the study the whole evening.

"I don't want to live just with him," Sarah said.

"He ought to get us—it's only fair," said Preston. "He hasn't done anything bad."

Elizabeth was bad and had done bad things. Sarah knew that. Sometimes when she and Preston came home from school, the house was empty. They went into the kitchen and ate cookies and drank milk and waited. And soon the telephone would ring and her mother would promise in her slurry voice to be home in thirty minutes. When Preston answered, he always asked for the phone number where she was. When she wasn't home in thirty minutes, which she usually wasn't, he called and asked when she would come. Thirty minutes, she always answered laughing, didn't I say thirty minutes.

Once while Preston was talking to their mother on the phone, Sarah's eyes suddenly filled with tears and when she reached for the glass of milk, she knocked it to the floor and it broke. When she tried to pick up the pieces, she cut a long gash on her forefinger, and soon there were swirls of blood and milk on the floor. Preston yelled that Sarah was bleeding to death. That time her mother came right home and bandaged Sarah's finger. Often after that, Sarah thought that if only she would cut her hand again, her mother would come home. But she could never bring herself to do it.

Early one morning about a month ago, while Preston and Sarah were eating breakfast in the kitchen, their mother came home and told their father that she had wrecked the car and had hurt someone. Through the crack at the hinge of the door, they could see her sitting on the ottoman with her head down, her hands clasped between her knees. Her face was pale, as though all the blood in her head had drained through the dark slash on her cheek. Their father sat stiff in the big chair, his hands gripping the arms. In a low voice, he said,

"I wish you had broken his neck instead of just his leg." He stood up and walked around the room a little and then stopped behind their mother. "Let me tell you something," he said. "Get it absolutely clear in your mind. This is the last chance you're going to have. Maybe almost killing your . . . friend has made you finally see what I've been telling you for the last two years. Okay. But this is your last chance. I won't let my life be utterly ruined by you. I won't let you ruin my children. You may need to destroy yourself—I don't understand stuff like that—but you won't destroy us."

At the beginning, when they had come to the rented house at the beach, their mother played with them in the sand. The very first day, she made an enormous reclining sand giant, with legs as long as the children's bodies and feet as tall as the children's legs. The giant had a nose the size of a grown man's fist and eyeballs as big as baseballs. Sarah and Preston gathered seaweed and when they asked to help her, Elizabeth sent them to the water's edge for buckets of water to keep the giant moist and into the high grass for flat blades to make a tunic for the giant.

That night, of course, the tide carried the giant out to sea, where, Elizabeth said, he joined Neptune's navy. The second day all the children begged for another giant and she made one. And again on the third day and on the fourth. But on the fifth day she said they were big enough to entertain themselves. After that, she sat under the umbrella on her little folding chair, her heels deep in the sand and her arms crossed. She seldom spoke but she didn't seem angry.

For the past week, though, she had begun to seem restless. Her anger flared at Sarah and Preston over the least thing, a cereal bowl left on a table, sand tracked in on the bottoms of their feet. After she yelled at them, she would grab them and hug them and say she was sorry and then plan something special to do, hunting blackberries at the point or walking down to the little store for candy and twice to the boardwalk in town for the special ice cream.

The second time, as they were walking along the boardwalk, they heard a man's voice calling her name. They went to the railing and looked down at the street. Just below them, a man sat on the fender of a little red car, waving a crutch and laughing in a loud way. His hair was gleaming white and his face was bright red and as he laughed his bright red tongue bounced in his mouth. Sarah knew that this was the man whose leg her mother had broken.

Without speaking, Elizabeth started to walk away. The man laughed again and said, "Aren't you even going to say you're sorry?"

Elizabeth came back to the railing and peered down. "I'm sorry," she said, "about a lot more than that."

"God, you're a cold one. Is that all I get?"

She didn't speak for a moment. Finally she said. "That's all," and walked away with Preston and Sarah.

That ruined the outing and the rest of the day. Elizabeth

made a big joke of choosing the flavor of ice cream, but they knew she was gloomy and unhappy. By the time they got back to their cottage, no one was speaking and they ate dinner in silence and went early to bed.

The next day Elizabeth went to the beach with them and stayed all day, only returning to the cottage to make sandwiches. She began a sand giant, but after she shaped the body she said they should finish it. She sat under the umbrella and stared at the sea. Back in the cottage that night, whenever a car passed on the gravel road, she stopped and listened. No one came.

Throughout the week she grew more and more restless and irritable. She began to stay inside and read or play solitaire while they went to the beach. Although Preston and Sarah never spoke of it, they took turns going back to the cottage—to go to the bathroom, to find a better sandpail, to get a cookie. And when they returned, they would answer the unspoken question with a slight nod—she's still all right.

She seemed to like the beach at night and after supper she left the house and walked alone from the dock to the point and back, her hands in the pockets of her windbreaker, her head lowered, looking—Sarah thought as she watched her from the darkened screen porch—as though she were searching for something lost in the sand. Once Preston asked if she had seen anyone on the beach. Her face flamed and her lips curled into her teeth. She said, "Are you the CIA or the FBI or just his private little snoop?"

Preston grabbed his tongue with his back teeth and chewed a little. Elizabeth started out of the house again but when she got to the bottom of the steps she stopped. She stood without moving for a moment and then she turned and ran back up the steps. She grabbed Preston and made him sit on her lap in the wicker rocker on the screen porch. "You're my babies," she said, rocking Preston as if he really were a baby. "You're all I care about." She drew Sarah to her and hugged and kissed her.

Sarah stared down into the water at the jellyfish, swirling against the rocks. It was Friday and their father would be down late that evening. She imagined the headlights of her father's car swirling in the dark fog and then the frosted bottle on the drainboard and her mother at the kitchen table with the sick-laughing look on her face and the man with the bright red tongue. She will, Sarah said to herself, I already know.

She looked at the jellyfish. She imagined the jellyfish floating against her legs and then the feel of the slime and the sharp prickles. She saw herself get out of the water and run as quickly as she could up to the cottage, crying. Her mother's hand was on the bottle and the red-faced man was laughing, his tongue bouncing in his mouth. Her mother saw the welts on Sarah's legs and she put down the glass and took Sarah into the bathroom and washed off the slime. The man drove away in the little red car and her father drove up.

"There's a jellyfish," she said. Preston looked where she pointed.

"Two of them," he said. "Over there's another." Near the piling where it was deep enough to dive was another pink mass.

"Do you think I ought to go swimming?" she asked.

"God, you're dumb," said Preston.

For a moment she thought she would tell him, but then she saw children running down the road and coming out to the dock. He probably wouldn't understand and he would laugh at her and tell the other children. She said, "That was a joke."

When they went to the cottage at lunchtime, they found Elizabeth lying on the wicker sofa, staring at the ceiling.

"What's wrong?" asked Preston. He peered around the kitchen door and Sarah did too. There was no bottle. Elizabeth stood up.

"Nothing's wrong," she said. "How could anything be wrong in this peachy little cottage at the peachy little beachy? And with your sainted father coming tonight, why, all is pure heaven."

Sarah said, "There were two jellyfish."

Preston said, "And she was going to go swimming."

"I was not, I was not," she cried, and then the hot tears were burning her eyes and her cheeks. She felt her mother's arms come around her and she smelled the soap and the hand lotion and something else just her mother's, but there was no smell of drink.

"Poor lamb," Elizabeth said. "Cries and cries and doesn't even know why. Don't worry, I know you wouldn't get into a fight with a couple of jellyfish. What kind of odds are those, Preston? What chance has a mere mortal against a couple of primordials?"

All afternoon, Sarah waited for it to happen. She came up from the beach three or four times to check. Once Elizabeth was in the bedroom and she went in. Elizabeth had taken off her shorts and shirt and had on a pink cotton dress. She was fixing her hair.

"Are you going to visit the people next door?" Sarah asked.

"They went back to the city," Elizabeth said.

"Did you make friends with the people down the road with the Jeep station wagon?"

"Oh, God, baby, not even your father can stand them. She has adenoids and he wears perforated shoes."

Sarah said, "Do you want me to walk to the village with you?"

"Because I've put on this dress?" Elizabeth asked, smiling. "Such a curious little lamb and so subtle with her questions. I just thought I'd been such a bitch all day that I'd dress up and try to act like a nice lady for a change. Okay?"

When Sarah got back to the beach, Preston told her he was going to the point for blackberries and she could come if she helped him get the canoe into the water. He lifted the tip of the canoe out of the high grass where they moored it and motioned for her to pick up the other end. She tried but she couldn't get a good grip on it.

"I'll do it by myself," he said irritably, "and you can't go with me, either."

She said, "I think she's started."

Preston dropped the tip of the canoe and straightened up. He began to chew his tongue. He looked down the beach and up the gravel road toward the cottage. "You going with me or not? You could at least push."

54

Once they got the canoe into the water, Sarah sat behind and Preston in front. When she lifted her paddle to change sides, she flicked water on his back, but he didn't complain. She hadn't really lied to him. All she had said was that she thought it had started. She stopped paddling and trailed her hand in the water. She saw the dark blue and silver-gray stones embedded in the sand and a few fish, a silver twist in the water and then gone.

"Did you call Daddy?" Preston asked.

"About what?"

"We weren't supposed to stay by ourselves. We were supposed to call him if it happened."

"What happened?" she asked. Preston twisted a little and stared at her over his shoulder. And she knew. "I said think. I didn't say it already had. And I didn't call because he's coming anyway. So there."

Preston sat the paddle down in the bottom of the boat and swiveled on his bottom to face her. "You made it up," he said. "You lied."

"I didn't mean to," she answered. "It just came out because I know it will. I can tell. I see pictures."

"I got a great mind to dump you out of the boat."

"I'll jump!" she yelled. She stood up and waved her arms wildly. She would drown and he would run back to the house to tell about it and he would get there just in time and it wouldn't happen. But then no one would know she had stopped it.

"Sit down!" Preston shouted. "You'll upset the boat."

She sat down and said quietly, "It's true. You'll see."

"You're just a liar," he said. He started paddling again.

When they got to the point, he pulled the canoe up to the beach and picked up the pail and started walking off. He didn't wait for her.

The best blackberries were on the far side of a barbed-wire fence and across a little creek. Preston spread the strands of the wire and ducked between. Then without looking at her, he waited to help her. He pressed down on the lower strand with his foot and pulled up the upper strand.

"I can do it by myself," she said. "You're not very nice." When he let go, the strands sang for a moment.

She couldn't remember how he had gone through but she wouldn't ask. She knew he had used a foot and a hand. But when she tried to do that, and to balance one foot on the wire while she brought the other leg through, the wire sprang away. A barb caught just below her knee and ripped up her leg. She heard a harsh howl, like a cat in a fight.

Preston dropped the pail and ran back. She had fallen to the ground and was clutching her shin. Blood spurted out onto her hands. Preston said, "Why didn't you let me help you, you should have let me help you." He peered at the wound, at the blood flowing down her leg. He looked desperately around, as if help might come from the woods or the creek. "We better wash it," he said. He picked up the bucket and ran to the creek. "Please stop crying," he called.

He brought the pail of water and poured it over the wound and she yelped with the pain. The water and the blood pooling in her sneaker were cold and slimy. Preston took off his shirt and ripped it into strips. He tied one strip into a big knot at the back of her knee and he bound the wound with the other strips. She was so surprised and pleased at how much he knew to do for her that she forgot about the blood oozing through the bandage and the slime and the pain.

"Mom better look at it," he said. He held her elbow as they walked back to where they had beached the canoe and he helped her climb in and settle on the bottom with her foot on the seat. As he paddled, he turned every now and then to see that she was all right. Everything about the day was changing, and she was sure that it hadn't happened yet. She leaned over and stared into the water. No jellyfish. She could go swimming if she wanted.

By the time they got back to their beach, the wound had stopped bleeding. Preston told her to try not to bend her knee so that it wouldn't start up again. While Preston dragged the canoe into the grass, she walked stiff-legged up the hill. He caught up with her just as she rounded the corner into their part of the road.

Parked alongside their fence, half-blocking their little blue gate, was the little red car. They looked at the cottage and then at each other. Preston began to chew his tongue. After a moment, he went over to examine the car.

"Nifty," he said. "I'm going to have one of these someday." He looked inside the car and then back at the cottage. "Mine's going to be silver with black upholstery."

"Daddy says you're not to bite your tongue," said Sarah.

"I'm not," he answered. "I'm just thinking. I may have red upholstery." He kicked the wheels of the car and climbed on the bumper and bounced up and down. "You don't need me anymore, do you? I told those guys I'd meet them back at the beach." He wouldn't look her in the eye. "So long. I hope your leg's okay and all."

When he got to the turn in the road, she called, "See—I'm not a liar." He didn't stop.

Her mother sat on the wicker sofa with the man beside her. His leg in its thick cast rested on the coffee table. He had on light slacks and a plaid short-sleeved shirt open almost to his belt.

"Come here, lamb," Elizabeth said. She held her hand toward Sarah.

"What?" Sarah asked. She wanted her mother to speak again—she wasn't sure she had heard the bad voice, the slurring.

Elizabeth said, "Come over here and meet a friend who just happened to be passing this way." She spoke as if she had caught her tongue in her teeth, the way Preston did. But it wasn't that, it was drink.

"Hi, how you doing," the man said. "Hey, what'd you do to your knee?"

Sarah's eyes filled and heat flooded through her chest. She ran out of the living room and across the hall to her own room and threw herself down on the bed. She stuffed the pillow in her mouth so her mother would not hear her crying. She didn't want her mother to touch her, to ever touch her again. Her mother had lied and broken her promise. She had had her last chance. As soon as Preston came up from the beach, they would call their father. Her mother would never see any of them again. Her mother was bad and shouldn't be allowed to ruin them all.

For a second she thought her mother wasn't even going to come to look at the leg. And then she felt the side of the bed go down and felt her mother's hand on her neck. Sarah jerked away to the far edge of the bed.

Elizabeth's hand followed her, the fingers kneading her shoulders and then the knuckles walking up and down Sarah's spine. "Come on, precious girl," Elizabeth said, "let me take a look at that leg." She pulled until Sarah was lying on her back. She unwound Preston's bandages. When she lifted off the last layer, Sarah cried out because the bandage had stuck to the wound.

"That's a nasty cut," Elizabeth said in her slurred voice. "How did it happen?"

"I won't ever tell you," Sarah shouted. "I know why you put on that pink dress—you knew he was coming. You're just a liar!"

"Oh, no," Elizabeth said. "He was just in the neighborhood. Honest."

Elizabeth brought a saucepan of water from the kitchen and washed the knee and the leg and then slipped off the slimy sneaker and washed Sarah's foot. Then she put a greasy medicine on the wound and a real bandage of gauze and tape.

"There, precious girl," she said, "does that feel all better now?" Sarah nodded. She thought that Elizabeth's voice sounded all right now. Perhaps she had been wrong about the drink. "Want me to rock you?" Elizabeth asked.

Sarah sat up so that Elizabeth could lift her. She was glad it had happened, even though her knee still hurt a little. When they passed through the living room, she remembered the man. He was still sitting on the sofa, his leg in its cast propped on the coffee table. He shook his empty glass at them.

"How long can it take to fix a little bitty knee like that?" he asked, grinning.

Elizabeth said, "Fix yourself another drink."

When they were settled in the rocker on the porch, Sarah whispered, "He's not supposed to be here. And Daddy's coming."

"Poor little lamb," said Elizabeth. "Don't worry so. I'll make him leave soon."

"Do you promise?"

"I promise. But I don't want to be impolite, do I?"

Elizabeth began to sing softly to her and to pat her in time to the music. Sarah heard the distant voices of children, carried up from the beach on the surf. Preston and his friends. Preston would be glad she had made everything all right. The beach was a wonderful place. So blue and white, and the blue-green water and floating on the water in a little silver canoe peering down at the jellyfish and the silver fish. She turned her face into her mother's soft body, rising and falling with the song. She was floating, drifting with the song.

The singing went on and on and became soft music and the murmur of voices in the living room and then the sound of a car crunching to a halt on the gravel road. It was twilight and she was lying on her bed. "Oh, Christ," she heard her mother say and then a door slammed and then she heard her father's voice. Bad things had happened while she slept and now it was too late. Her mother had had her last chance.

When she stood up, her knee began to throb and ache. She pressed her fingers against the wound and a sharp pain shot through her leg. She began to rip off the tape. If she could make it hurt bad enough, perhaps it wouldn't be her father after all.

Homecoming

Lenora is packing. Late in the afternoon she will fly to Jamaica where the sun is hot, the water blue, the tax laws favorable. She negotiates loans for corporations operating in underdeveloped countries, and she and her counterpart in a London bank are closing a deal. Once the negotiation is completed, they will spend the weekend on the beach, in nightclubs and cafés, in bed. She likes this man very much, as she discovered nearly a year ago when they first met.

As she packs, she gazes out at the new snow covering Gramercy Park. Even after nineteen years up north, she has not gotten used to the winters. Do all your snowing while I'm gone. She sees herself oiled and tranquil in the hot sun.

The telephone rings. It is probably her boss with some big-deal idea that can't wait until Monday. Angus is already in the air, flying to Jamaica. Should she answer the phone? She then asks herself the question, If I were a man, would I or wouldn't I? That has been her standard ever since she was graduated from Agnes Scott College and set out to be a success in the great world. Would a man? She answers the telephone.

"Lenora? It's Edwin." Edwin is married to Lenora's sister, Joan. They still live in Macon.

"Why, Edwin, what brings you to New York?" she says in the slightly mocking voice she uses with him when she visits Macon. In the silence she hears the long-distance winds whistling along the wires. "Is anything wrong?" She knows. "Say it," she shouts. "She's dead, isn't she? Momma's dead!"

Edwin says something about a heart attack, something about doctors, something about doing all they could, but Lenora hardly hears him. The voice obliterated. The touch gone. Blood rushes to her head, and she holds tight to the phone.

"Are you all right?" Edwin asks. "Perhaps you ought to call someone. Can you call a friend?"

Lenora is close to many people—women friends from her first years in New York, a former lover she still has dinner with once a month, a man at her office with whom she goes to the opera and the ballet, others she loves and feels loved by. But she doesn't want to call them. They have never even met her mother. How can they know? After a moment, she says, "I'm all right now." She begins to make plans. "I'll fly in this afternoon. Don't bother to meet me—I'll take a taxi from the airport. And don't bother with a hotel—I'll just stay at Momma's." Her voice breaks on the word.

"Oh, no," says Edwin. "Joan and I want you with us."

"I'll just stay at Momma's," she repeats in a firm, soft voice. She doesn't want to stay at Joan's, in Joan's house of pale silks and delicate antiques inherited from Edwin's family. "Thanks, though."

When she hangs up, she takes a message pad from the bed-side table and jots notes to herself. Ask her secretary to book a flight to Atlanta that meshes with one in Macon. Cancel a lunch date. Phone her assistant and brief him so that he can go to Jamaica. She thinks how surprised Angus will be when the young man shows up. She'll call Angus after she gets to Macon.

She feels very cold, and she jerks the Moroccan spread off the bed and wraps it around her shoulders. She walks to the window and rests her head against the metal frame. As the snow floats by, she remembers the blizzard when she was eleven, when Macon was nearly paralyzed for three days. No stores open, no school. She sees herself at the kitchen win-dow, peering through the quarter moon she had cleared in the fogged glass. The snow is as thick as summer rain, but she can see the shadowy form of her mother dragging an immense tarpaulin across the narrow field to protect the rose bushes— growing roses was her mother's latest idea for making a little extra money. Lenora remembers that almost all the bushes broke under the weight of the heavy canvas and the still fall-ing snow. She turns away from the window, tosses the spread over a chair, and begins to repack. She will need warm clothes. It is remarkable, she thinks, how otherwise informed people believe Georgia is in the tropics.

In the early evening the taxi deposits Lenora in the narrow dirt driveway beside her mother's house. The house is a dinky box, two rooms wide, two deep, and two tall, at least on the front. The taxi's headlights illuminate the field where the rose bushes were. She remembers that another summer they used the field to grow vegetables to sell. A man with cotton-colored hair dangled a corn worm over her head, and her mother pushed his hand away, saying, She's sensitive, don't tease her.

The front door is unlocked, and she steps silently into the little hall. She hears the murmur of voices and the chink of cups against saucers. When her nostrils clear of the cold outside air, she smells the familiar odors—the lilac cologne, the lemon wax, the Cashmere Bouquet. Lady smells. She tosses her coat over the needlepoint bench and walks to the living-room door.

The voices subside. Forms rise to greet her. For one instant she forgets—she waits expectantly. But when she feels Joan's hand on her arm and Joan's breath on her cheek, she acknowledges that their mother is not—cannot be—among these people. For a moment she feels dizzy, crazy. She grabs Joan's shoulder.

"We'll talk in the dining room," Joan whispers.

Lenora straightens. "What is there to say?" she asks. She moves away and looks at Joan. Joan is in her middle forties, four years older than Lenora. Her dark hair is beginning to gray, and she wears it in a soft curve around her face. She is wearing a plum-colored suit and a multicolored blouse that picks up the plum. She is pretty, graceful, feminine, even in a suit. Lenora smiles and says, "Anne Klein?" and points to the suit.

All evening people come and go. Elderly strangers, cousins Lenora has forgotten that she owned, friends of Joan's and Edwin's, the minister. Joan greets everyone and accepts the offerings of condolence—a ham, chrysanthemums, a pound cake, a bottle of Bristol Cream Sherry. Joan introduces people to Lenora. You remember Lenora. Lenora flew in this evening from New York. Someone whispers to Joan. Joan says, "She hadn't come yet."

Lenora sits in the rocker in front of the false fireplace. The room is dull and stiff. The chairs and sofa are rose and dull pink. They are tightly upholstered so that there is no give to them. They are meant to wear and last. Lenora thinks about her apartment, the soft leathers, the bright rich colors, the view of the park. Her mother had never seen the apartment. I'm too old to figure out that city.

The minister smiles at Lenora from across the room. "You look just like your momma, sitting in that rocker." Lenora smiles back.

"Actually," says one of the cousins, "I think Joan looks more like her. Joan has Aunt Emily's smile."

"Thank you," says Joan.

"You're right," says the minister, "but their momma always sat in that rocker, knitting those lovely sweaters."

Lenora sees the yarn pouring through her mother's fingers into sweaters she sold to the town's rich women. More pennies. After a minute, Lenora moves to the sofa. She waits for Joan to sit in the rocker, but Joan doesn't.

The pound cake is on the end table, and Lenora cuts a thin slice and pours a glass of sherry. She has had nothing to eat since lunch except a soggy sandwich at the Atlanta airport. Soon Edwin helps an old woman lower her bulk to the sofa. Edwin eases her down as though she were breakable. He is a stockbroker, and the old woman is probably one of his clientele of widows. When Lenora tells her stockbroker friends about Edwin, she says he is a big gray sheepdog and the old woman are his sheep and he does not want them fleeced.

The woman has blue hair and bright red circles on her cheeks, and her breath smells like sour milk. She looks intently at Lenora, and her eyes fill. "How old was Emily?" she asks in a low conspiratorial tone.

"Seventy-one," says Lenora. Only seventy-one.

The old woman's face lights up, and she slaps Lenora's knee. "I'll be eighty-two next month," she almost shrieks.

"You don't look it," Lenora responds. The old woman smiles contently. Lenora wonders what eighty-two looks like.

The old woman begins to talk in a steady flow. She says the town will miss Emily. Emily was a good woman. She says Emily used to arrange the flowers and make the dessert when the old woman gave a party. She says of course she always gave Emily a little something for it. Poor Emily, she says, how she skimped and saved to send Joan and Lenora to Agnes Scott. She wonders if Lenora knows that things got a lot easier toward the end because Edwin gave Emily money each month. Lenora wonders, silently, if the old woman knows that she did, too. The old woman says she doesn't know what Emily would have done without Edwin and Joan.

"I don't, either" says Lenora. "Would you like some pound cake?"

"I never eat late in the evening," the old woman whispers, thumping her belly with her fists. "It gives me gas pains."

"Me, too," says Lenora, breaking off a corner of the cake and putting it in her mouth. The old woman sighs and presses the heels of her hands against her thighs and tries to stand. Joan hurries over and hauls her to her feet.

The old woman says, "Well, I'll see you girls tomorrow. When did you say the service was?"

"I wouldn't know," says Lenora. "Ask Joan."

"Two o'clock," says Joan.

Everyone but the family has gone. Lenora feels uneasy, restless. "I was going to fly to Jamaica this afternoon. You just caught me, in fact."

"I hear it's beautiful there," Edwin says. Lenora thinks of Edwin in his gray three-piece suit and white shirt and dark tie, lying on the beach. Or would he wear a little gray bikini? Lenora smiles. She remembers Angus on the beach, lean and tall. She wonders if Jamaica is on Eastern time. Edwin says, "This summer we were going to take your mother to Sea Island on our vacation."

"It wasn't a vacation, it was business," Lenora says quickly. "Of course, if I'd known anything was wrong . . ."

"She asked me not to tell you," Joan says.

"Not to tell me what?"

"That she was sick," says Joan.

Lenora stands up. She has assumed the heart attack was sudden, death almost immediate. She walks to the glass-front china cabinet where her mother kept her pink demitasse cups and the silver service. "And how long was she sick?" she asks. She opens the door and lifts the top off the sugar bowl. She moves the creamer a quarter of an inch to the right and pulls the teapot forward.

"She was in the hospital for five days."

Lenora blows on the little cups. There is no dust. "Did I hear right? Five days?"

Joan says, "She had a little something first, and the doctor wanted to run some tests, and so he kept her in the hospital."

"And you didn't call me," says Lenora. It is half assertion, half question. In the mirror at the back of the cabinet she sees Edwin and Joan exchange glances.

"The doctor didn't think it amounted to anything, and she didn't want you to think you had to come charging down here."

Now Lenora moves the creamer back an inch. The pieces seem in balance. "You mean, wouldn't want to come? Even though my mother was in the hospital?"

"Not that, of course," says Joan. "But your job. She was awfully proud of that. You were her big success." She smiles. "Her pride."

"And you her comfort," says Lenora. She fingers the teapot. She remembers so many times waking up alone in the room she shared with Joan and realizing that Joan was with their mother, talking, talking. Comforting. There is a big dent in the side of the pot, and Lenora remembers that when she had used it in a junior high school musical two boys had played football with it. Her mother had said never mind the dent because it would be Lenora's some day and Lenora would be rich enough to have it mended. "Momma said she would leave this to me."

65

"Take anything you want," says Joan.

Joan dispensing the remains. "If I want, I will," says Lenora. She forces a laugh. She knows Edwin and Joan are shooting looks at each other. She closes the cabinet, walks to the doorway, and glances up the cramped dark staircase. Two sharp turns and at the top the two bedrooms and the hall bathroom that smelled a little of mildew.

"I never spent the night here alone," she says.

"You won't have to," says Joan. "I'm going to stay here with you tonight."

"That won't be necessary," says Lenora.

Edwin looks from one to the other. "If Lenora doesn't particularly want you here, why not come home with me now?"

Joan waves her hand impatiently. "I told you I want to stay in this house tonight. With my sister."

Lenora says, "I can stay alone. I'm a big girl now."

She waits for Joan to say, Then act like one. Joan says, "I'm not doing it for you. I've already made up the beds. You can stay in our old room."

"And you in Momma's," says Lenora. She won't wait for a response. She fakes a stretch and a yawn. "I don't care where I sleep just so long as I start doing it fairly soon."

"I'm leaving, then," says Edwin. "Tomorrow's going to be rough. You girls better get some rest."

"I'm not a girl," says Lenora. "I'm a banker."

Edwin smiles benignly. "Sorry—I thought you just said you were a big girl now."

Joan's eyes gleam. She holds up her face to receive Edwin's kiss. Lenora laughs and says, "Baaa."

Now the sisters are alone. Joan sits in the rocker, one knee across the other knee, her hands holding each other in her lap. Lenora sits on the sofa. She is in a dangerous condition and she knows it. "Did you say the service was at two?"

"Yes, at All Saints. Remember All Saints?" Joan smiles ruefully.

"How could I forget. Didn't Momma do the altar flowers

66

there?" There is a little fire kindled deep inside her and she wants it to flame. She adds, "Wasn't that one of her shit jobs?"

Joan's smile drops. "I wouldn't call it that. She certainly wouldn't."

I'm not too proud to make a little money any honest way I can. Lenora's throat hardens, but she won't take back the ugly word, not for Joan. She shrugs. "And after All Saints?"

"Burial at Elmwood," says Joan. She pinches her eyes closed. After a moment she says, "I'm awfully tired. Let's go to bed."

Lenora doesn't want Joan to leave yet. She cocks her head and says, "Did I forfeit my rights as daughter by moving to New York?"

Joan looks at Lenora. "What does that mean?"

"Why wasn't I consulted about anything?" asks Lenora. Her voice is all control, all reasonableness. She manages a quizzical little smile.

"You were thirty thousand feet up in the air," says Joan. "How could we consult you?" Now Joan lowers her gaze and examines a cuticle. She looks up at Lenora. "I'm sorry if you're upset about it. It isn't too late. Anything you don't like we can change. Edwin will take you down to the mortuary in the morning."

Lenora does not want to go to the mortuary. She does not want to see the casket. She does not want to look inside.

"It's the principle," she says. "I don't give a damn whether it's a bronze casket with blue satin or a wooden casket with white. I just want to be consulted. You didn't even ask me whether I wanted her body buried or cremated."

"She made that decision herself a long time ago. I'm surprised she didn't tell you. She told me often enough."

"Of course she would tell you," says Lenora. Was that the kind of thing they talked about in the big bed late at night? I want my body buried, honey, you see to it. "You should have told me she was sick, goddammit. You owed me that at least."

Joan sighs and pushes at another cuticle. "I'm really sorry you feel that way. I did what I thought was best."

67

"Don't you always and is it ever?" says Lenora.

"Of course if I'd known what was going to happen, I'd have called you right away."

Now the flame leaps. "You knew," says Lenora. "You knew damn well."

"Of course I didn't." Joan stands abruptly. "How could I have?"

"Maybe not up here," says Lenora tapping her forehead with her forefinger, "but somewhere back here," cupping the back of her skull, "you knew all right. You didn't call me because you wanted her all to yourself. Her comfort all the way."

"That's crazy, you're crazy," says Joan. "I didn't call you because she asked me not to."

"And you always did everything she asked."

"More than some," Joan shoots back.

Suddenly they grow silent, listening. They can hear the hum of the refrigerator, the muffled roar of the furnace, the slamming of a car door in the distance. Nothing else. She won't come this time, her voice, her touch, soothing, bringing peace. They know that. They're on their own now.

Joan digs her fingers into her eye sockets. Lenora stands.

"See you in the morning," she says softly.

Lenora switches on the overhead light in the room she had shared with Joan. The room is just the same. The wallpaper is immense cabbage roses and spiraling pale green vines. The bedspread is a dusty pink chenille, and the curtains are pink cretonne. Pink and rose. Her mother's favorite colors. Lady colors.

She sits down on the dressing table stool. There are empty vials of perfume and atomizers covered with silky pink threads. There is the old Schiaparelli Shocking she had given Joan one Christmas and the Chanel No. 5 Joan had given her. There is a Jergen's Lotion bottle with a hard crust around its neck. She doesn't remember whether that was hers or Joan's. She picks up a cardboard box of dusting powder, and when she removes the top a cloud of dust settles on the glass surface of the table. Was the powder hers or Joan's?

68

When she wipes the powder off with a tissue, she notices that the photographs are still under the glass. She hasn't looked at them for twenty years. She turns on the dressing table lamp to see them better. Herself on a pony. Joan with a frizzy new permanent. Joan in a cap and gown. Herself in a cap and gown.

She moves some vials and jars. Her father in his dark Marine uniform, Joan holding his hand and Lenora perched on his shoulder. And then a later picture of him with a little Japanese woman and a baby. Her picture, not Joan's. She remembers once Joan tried to pick out the picture with a nail file. And her mother saying I don't mind if Lenora has the picture—he is her father. That was all her mother ever said about it. Was that what her mother and Joan talked about in the double bed? Her father's new life? The letter Lenora had written him?

In the middle of the dressing table is a little glass tray with a tarnished brass fence around it and an ivory-handled manicure set on it. Lenora pushes the tray aside. There is a picture of her mother and Joan and a man in a fedora hat, standing in front of a car with a wrap-around windshield. She doesn't recognize the man. In another picture there is a blond man in droopy bathing shorts, with one hand clasping her mother's bare shoulder and the other resting on Lenora's head. Is it the man who had teased her with the corn worm? She must have been six or seven then. There is another picture of the blond man, pushing her mother in a wheelbarrow, and her mother is laughing. She doesn't remember her mother laughing like that. Who are these men? Were they her lovers? She never thinks of her mother that way, never thinks of her as young and having fun. She always sees her knitting those sweaters, planting the ill-fated roses, concocting special desserts. Shit work. So that her daughters could go to Agnes Scott, so that Joan could marry one of the town's most eligible young men and Lenora could be a banker and make lots of money and travel and enjoy life.

She remembers Angus, and she wonders if it is too late to call him. Would a man call this late? she asks herself. She laughs silently. Now she cocks the lampshade so that the light reflects directly on her face. She plucks at the flesh under her eyes and stretches smooth the edges of her lips. She smiles. She thinks her smile is as much like her mother's as Joan's is. She has her mother's gray eyes and her mother's full lips and the same chin. Joan has the forehead and the cheekbones and the shape of the eyes.

Does Joan know who the men in the photographs are and what happened to them? Probably. Joan always knew more. Four years did that. And no matter how hard Lenora tried, she could never catch up. Naturally Joan was closer.

Not closer, she hears her mother whisper. Just different. Joan's my big girl. You're my baby.

Abruptly Lenora stands up and goes to her suitcase. She takes out the nightgown and dressing gown she had placed on top. Just below is the dark green suit brought for the service. She shakes it out and hangs it in the chiffonier. It won't need pressing—it's a good traveling suit. About as good as an Anne Klein, she thinks.

She undresses and gets into the twin bed. She is so tired that she expects to fall right to sleep. But she can't get settled. She decides it is because she is used to an electric blanket, not layers of cotton quilts. She remembers that when she was restless and couldn't sleep, she too would go and get in bed with her mother, and they too would talk and talk. She remembers lying on her side, fitted against her mother as though she were sitting in her mother's lap. She remembers her mother's knees against the backs of hers, her mother's arms across her waist, her mother's breasts against her back, her mother's warm damp breath on the back of her neck. Close, warm in the darkness.

Lenora doubles up her fists and presses them between her thighs. She has forgotten how cold Macon can be in the winter at night. She begins to shake with the terrible chill.

She gets out of bed and walks down the hall to her mother's bedroom. When she opens the door, Joan sits up in bed. Joan whispers, "What is it? What do you want?"

70

Lenora can't speak, but she knows she doesn't need to. She walks over to the bed and sits down. She feels Joan's hand on her arm. She gets under the covers. The two women face each other, their knees touching, their foreheads touching. They reach out and grasp each other's hands until the bones ache. Grief hurtles back and forth between them like an electric current. They hold each other through the night.

The Waiting Game

He sat in his book-lined office. The only sound was the little pop! when the paper clips he twisted gave way. He tried to imagine the scene in the Common Room below. The faculty members extracted tuna sandwiches from brown sacks, stirred coffee, sipped, crossed and recrossed their legs, ruminated. About him. Was he or was he not good enough to join their illustrious—and don't forget secure—ranks as an associate professor?

I most certainly am good enough, Thomas Kincaid shouted silently. I am just goddam good. First rate. Tops. Who the hell could doubt such an obvious fact? He jumped to his feet. Who? Who? As though in answer, faces of his colleagues loomed forth from the shadows in the corners of his office: old man Cathcart, Peggy Bates, Tony Petters, Millette, Grobstein, Ramsay . . . all smug, hostile, doubting. Abruptly he sat down and picked up another paper clip.

Thirty of them against only one of him was so unfair. And he wasn't even allowed to defend himself. They could fire him without even listening to what he had to say. Star Chamber. The promotion committee would present his case, and then the others would grade, weigh, hack, trim, and slice the poor carcass. Of course, his special pals, Peggy Bates and Millette, would argue for him. They had assured him of that. They claimed they would win. And as they explained just how they would win, they seemed to imply that without their cunning political sense and perhaps even trickery, his case was hopeless.

Friends. Kincaid broke another paper clip. All those two cared about was power, politics, trying to rule the department. He and Harriet had no friends. Except maybe Harriet's tennis partners. Six years on the faculty, and not one person really gave a damn about him. Not one.

All right now, he cautioned himself, pretend you are a fair, sane, reasonable person. Only that morning, Peggy had come sailing into his office, with two cups of her famous espresso, a sack of sweet rolls, and cheery words of confidence—it's a cinch, leave it to us. As she dripped sugar glaze down her chin onto her immense expanse of pale blue cashmere and ticked off the names of his die-hard supporters, she had whipped his anxiety into a frenzy. It would have been better if she had stayed away. Still, she meant well. He guessed.

Someone was playing tunes on the carillon, and Kincaid walked to the window. The sun glinted on the red tile roofs across the Quad. Eucalyptus trees swayed and rustled in the slight wind. Young men and women walked in twos and fours along the shadowed arcades. A few people were eating lunch in the little oasis of trees and flowers in the middle of the Quad. Three large men in dark business suits burst from the Administration Building and strode off, laughing, gesticulating, toward the Faculty Club. A pleasant place. A nice life. He sighed.

He glanced at his wristwatch. It was twenty minutes before one. Better get some lunch in him so he would be able to take it when Cathcart came bearing the evil tidings. He drew on his jacket, straightened his necktie, with his fingertips punched a relaxed expression around his mouth, and went out into the sunlight.

The path he took curved between the church and the Common Room, and suddenly he realized he was within twenty-five feet of where the faculty meeting was taking place. His peripheral vision picked up movement in the window. They would think he had hidden in the bushes, snooping, eavesdropping. Should he run back to his office? keep going as nonchalantly as possible? turn and acknowledge them? faint? He pretended to study the inscription carved into the sandstone buttress of the ludicrous church: "Partially destroyed 1906—Restored 1913."

And recalled saying, not six months ago, that it was a rotten shame they'd restored the monstrous thing. God a'mighty, said it to old Billy Cathcart whose entire life man and boy had been spent in the shadow of that church. He remembered that he and Harriet had gone to the Cathcarts for their yearly dinner. To wash down the main course of shreds of beef and hunks of gristle, he had drunk an enormous quantity of red jug wine and had expanded into confidentiality.

"That's the damndest structure I've ever seen. Guy who designed it couldn't decide whether he was building a Byzantine mosque, a classical temple, or a Gothic cathedral. What an abortion." And he had bubbled with laughter.

The old man had cut a look at him. "So you don't like our looks? A great many don't." And then the mirthless laugh. "Hunhunhun," in which Kincaid heard a dirge: "They aren't here anymore."

"As much as telling me I wouldn't make tenure," Kincaid had said to Harriet as they were getting ready for bed that night.

"Doesn't sound like that to me," said Harriet.

"You should have heard him. His voice was like ice."

"Anyway, he's just the chairman," she called. "He doesn't own the place."

"That's what you think," said Kincaid. "Hunhunhun." Then he had dropped his shoulders forward in the Cathcart hunch, twisted his lip in the Cathcart grimace, cut a Cathcart look at Harriet under his eyebrows, and said in a pretty good imitation of Cathcart's voice, "The last ten fellows I fired didn't like the church either. Hunhunhun. No sense of true beauty. Hunhunhun. No sense of survival either." And soon, all anxiety forgotten, he and Harriet were roaring with laughter.

Maybe someday he would show the imitation to some of the younger faculty. He imagined Peggy shrieking, Millette howling. After he got tenure. "Hunhunhun," he said aloud, thrusting his head forward and pursing his lips. "Hunhunhun," he said to the inscription. And then remembering the shadow in the window of the Common Room, he turned to stare into the eyes of Billy Cathcart.

Heat blazed into Kincaid's brain. Concrete clogged his windpipe. Please, he said, I'll never do it again, not even for Harriet, only don't let the old man have understood. Let him think I'm just a loony talking to himself. Cathcart blinked, smiled, turned from the window.

The truth was, Kincaid thought, that despite the pretenses to the contrary—inviting him for lunch at the Faculty Club, appointing him to the most interesting committees—Cathcart had never liked him, never respected him. The old man spent his evenings, Sundays, holidays pouring over medieval manuscripts. He had written a lot of important monographs on etymologies, had chased obscure words down the centuries. He doubtless thought Kincaid's work was pop journalism, fit only to titillate middlebrows.

Now you listen, Kincaid said, turning back to the inscription and nodding, what I do is a lot more important than that moth-eaten comma-counting you call research. Ambrose Bierce, for God's sake. Fascinating. The artist who cast himself out. America's least-known great writer. Maybe. Anyway, I wrote a hell of a dissertation and a pretty darn good book. Sold nearly two thousand copies, practically a best seller for that kind of book.

He noticed movement in the window, and he turned just a little. Whereas you birds, he said, have achieved precious little. Grobstein had one article on Spenser in five years and most of the others rode around all year on a single book review. Peggy Bates hadn't written a word except letters to the editor since she discovered the sisterhood and stopped dieting. George Flemming wrote one short story a year and called himself a writer. And mad Arthur Casey hadn't had a graduate student in a decade, and the undergraduates avoided him in droves. Not that he wanted to knock poor Casey, but Casey sitting in judgment was a laugh. Who were they to deny him tenure? God, maybe he'd deny them tenure, retroactively.

Angrily, he focused on the windows again. And saw Tony Petters peering out at him. Peering back, Kincaid saw three books by Petters, all important, all brilliant, daring, and yet

75

no one caught him on a single detail. And Petters wasn't even forty-five yet. Such a mind. All over the place, synthesizing like hell, but like a knife, too.

Kincaid felt his shoulders sag a little. We can't all be super-stars, he said to the face in the window. We can't all have ten-ure, Petters answered in his phony British accent. Petters, in the window, smiled. Or was he laughing?

With all the dignity he could muster, Kincaid bowed slightly and walked off. Bastards. To hell with them. He was soon out of sight, and he began to walk quickly, almost running past the fountain behind the church. He certainly was not going to let them bother him. That telephone call from his friend teach-ing at Wisconsin: "Are you going to the MLA meeting at Christ-mas?" Actually he didn't care whether they voted him tenure or not. Way out here west of nowhere, north of nothing. Wis-consin. Now that was a university.

As he entered the Student Union, he decided he would call Harriet and tell her to get her mother's old fur coat out of moth balls. On Wisconsin, on Wisconsin, da duh da duhduh. He rummaged through the lint in his pocket and extricated a dime. He should have let Harriet come to the campus for lunch, as she had suggested. But he hadn't wanted anyone to think he needed his hand held, when he didn't. He dialed. Hello, darling, he practiced, just thought I'd tell you about Wisconsin. And then her rich voice easing along his nerves, kneading his flesh into jam.

When she hadn't picked up the phone by the third ring, he began to think she wasn't home. After he had specifically asked her not to leave the house, in case he needed her. What did she do all day long, anyway? Played a little tennis but mostly worked on her dissertation on Monet. She said. But if he asked her what she had done on the dissertation, she tensed and said, "Not much today," in a please-quit-nagging voice. On the sixth ring, he asked himself, What does she *really* do all day? And with whom?

Will you stop? he shouted. Wasn't it humiliating enough to be hysterical over his job without becoming utterly demented over his loyal, loving wife? God, he was such a mess. All his bad selves had come shouting at him, shoving, jostling. Suspicious Husband. Jealous Colleague. Hostile Friend. Obsequious Underling—was there no end to it?

Though he tried to stop counting the rings, he was sure the eighth had tolled. How long could it take to answer the phone in a one-bedroom apartment? She didn't care enough about him to stay home this day of all days. Probably off playing tennis. She knew sports made him feel inadequate, and yet she persisted. He was less important than her tennis pals. Big butch types with thick shoulders and angry whacks. Ten. Eleven. When he had met Harriet, she had been sharing an apartment in New York with a dumpy graduate student in anthropology. Wirey hair and crooked teeth. Why would Harriet have had such an unattractive roommate unless they were lovers?

When Harriet said, "Hello," he wasn't ready to forgive her all those long rings, or that unattractive roommate.

"Where the hell have you been?" he asked. "Playing tennis I bet with whom?"

"I was dumping the trash," she said. "You forgot last night."

"That's right," he shouted, "blame me. You can always make it my fault." His heart pounded in a glorious anger.

"I wasn't blaming you," she said quietly. "I was explaining. Look, take it easy. How's it going?"

"Ducky," he said, "just ducky. I am duckily taking it easy as you so duckily suggest, and everything is just ducky."

Her sigh floated into his ear. He wanted to make a joke, but his jaws were clamped shut, all sound locked inside his chest. But somewhere in his head a voice whispered, Please help.

She must have heard it. "Sweetheart," she murmured. "Darling."

With these words his bones dissolved, and he had to brace himself against the plastic walls of the telephone booth. "I'm not sure I can survive," he said. "I'm trembling. I've been hallucinating all day. Why, right in the middle of my class this morning, I had a hideous vision of Tony Petters in one of his Savile Row suits sitting in the back row, smirking at every word. You know he visited my class two weeks ago?"

"Petters likes you," said Harriet. "You said he said it was a terrific class."

"Well, I wish he really had been there today. I was positively brilliant. Non-stop sheer genius for fifty minutes." He smiled, remembering the keen looks on the faces of his students. Bright. Attentive. Admiring. "It was about the relationship between Poe and Melville. I had a fabulous new way to tie them together."

"You don't have to worry about Poe," she said. "You have Poe cold."

"I wasn't worried, Harriet," he said a little testily. "I said I was brilliant. I should write up this new idea."

"You wrote that article on Poe, you were on that Melville symposium," she said reassuringly. "You don't have to worry about them."

He allowed a long pause for his irritation to grow. "You aren't helping, Harriet," he said.

"God knows I'm trying," she answered. "I could do a lot better if you came home. We could make love, we could drink that champagne." He saw the two of them stretched on the bed with tulip-shaped champagne glasses puddling on their bare chests. "We could make up cruel rhyming couplets," she went on, "about the faculty and how tedious and pedantic they are and how much cleverer you are."

"You think I don't have a single friend on the entire faculty, don't you? You think I don't have a prayer . . ."

"Please," she murmured, "don't."

"That is exactly what you think, that not one of my colleagues has the least respect for my work, and you think that because you yourself don't respect . . ."

"Goddammit," she exploded with such force that his eardrums began to vibrate, "you just stop that right this minute." Something fell into place inside him. Harriet. She was there. She loved him.

He put his lips close to the mouthpiece of the telephone and whispered, "They love me, they adore me. They're taking so long because each must have a turn praising my virtues, my talents, my handsome face."

Mollified, she said, "In the meantime, why don't you bring that handsome face home."

He sighed. "Imagine the love-making, the state I'm in. Anyway, I'm okay now, doctor. Only will you please not take out any more trash in case I need to call you, and will you please *please* not go play tennis with that nexus of lesbians you pal around with."

"Darling," she said, "you're a real mess."

He pushed through the throng of students milling around the food counters of the cafeteria and took his place in the hamburger line. A young man, brushing by, said, "Hello, Professor Kincaid."

"Hello . . . yourself," Kincaid said. He knew the face but couldn't remember the name. He nodded, smiled, stepped forward in the line.

Well, that was one area where the faculty couldn't fault him. He was okay with students. He always stayed a few minutes after class in case a student had a question. Kept office hours meticulously. Had high standards and graded hard, but the students knew he was absolutely fair. Didn't try to fool around with the women students. Friendly, but correct right down the line. Not buddy-buddy like some he could name. Millette with his hordes, eating donuts every half hour at the Union. Ramsay prancing through the arcades with a half dozen students convulsed by his sallies. Mutual massaging of the egos—my disciple the student/my pal the professor. Ramsay hadn't published in fifteen years, and Millette even bragged about ad-libbing lectures. Yet they both had enormous classes.

Once Cathcart had said Kincaid's classes weren't drawing very well. "Only twelve in your Twain and James last quarter. Odd. The modern writers usually get big crowds of students these days."

"All the English majors have read *Huck Finn* five times already," Kincaid protested, "and God knows I can't make them love Henry James."

"Well, then, you better make them love Tom Kincaid . . . Hunhunhun," Cathcart had said. He had thrust his shoulder in the direction of the Administration Building across the Quad.

"Those fellows count students the way a miser counts gold. Every time I tell them we need to tenure someone, they haul out their computer print-outs and tell me we haven't the enrollments to justify it. So we better get them, eh? Hunhunhun."

Kincaid picked up a dripping carton of milk from the melting ice and a hamburger left cooling under the warming lamp. He squeezed some catsup on the hamburger, paid, and went in search of the student who had spoken to him.

He gazed around the vast dining hall. Blond hair, wasn't it? They all had blond hair. Red shirt? Whose wasn't? And then he saw the young man sitting half a dozen tables away, and all alone. What luck. Nice picture: him and a student chumming it up at the Union. Just like Millette. He worked his way around the chairs and tables.

"Hi," he said. The young man looked up over the book he had open before him. He folded the book over his index finger.

"Yeah?" he asked. He was a good-looking young man with dark blue eyes and a pale fuzz of moustache.

Kincaid sat down and slipped his hamburger out of the greased paper. "Want company while you eat?" he asked. Just saying it made him feel friendly and even boyish. Like Ramsay. He sank his teeth into the hamburger. In his free hand he caught the spurt of catsup and a little broken-off disc of bun.

For a few minutes he was fully occupied keeping the hamburger sufficiently together to eat it. When he had it under control, he looked up. The young man had his hands flat on the table and when he caught Kincaid's eye, smiled and stood up.

"I've got a midterm at two-fifteen," he said. "I can't afford another C after the one I got in Twain and James. Some other time, maybe?" He picked up his books and walked out of the cafeteria.

Kincaid tore open the milk carton and pinched off the paper wrapper around the straw. The truth was that he was lousy with students. He couldn't even remember their names, although he only had—what was it Cathcart had said?—twelve in a class. When they came into his office, he always felt tongue-tied and cross-eyed and prayed they'd go away. And they never stayed more than just long enough to get the assignment. They never invited him to the dorms for dinner, they never asked him to go for coffee. Had he really felt superior to Millette, contemptuous of Ramsay? He plunged his straw into the milk.

Maybe he wasn't one of the most popular professors, but he had good ideas and the students saw the mind stretched and grappling, not just spewing out old stuff. And what else was teaching all about? That morning, the wonderful moment when the idea about Poe and Melville had come to him. Original. Authentic. He took another bite of hamburger and washed it down with milk.

And then he couldn't remember what the idea had been. With the hamburger poised against his lips, he reconstructed the class. Poe's theories about the short story. Then to Hawthorne, and Hawthorne had leaped to Melville and Melville had reversed to Poe. But how? How? My God, it was like the dream-world—a glorious idea emerges as clear as crystal, but when you wake up it has vanished forever. Unless one of the students had taken careful notes on it. The red-faced girl with the long thin blond hair had fallen asleep for the eighth straight day, and the tall basketball player with the golden retriever at his heels hadn't shown up at all. Maybe he could ask the southern boy who sat in the front row and filled page after page with notes. I nevuh hud an original insight in this class, suh, he heard the boy say.

For of course there had never been an insight. Not really. An absurd conceit, perhaps, that could not stand the light of recollection. But no mind had stretched and grappled. Once again he had pretended to be what he was not. And right now the faculty was ripping off his disguises one by one. Scholar. Teacher. Colleague. Later in the afternoon, Cathcart would come taptaptapping at his chamber door and whisper Nevermore. And then for the next year while he was still on the payroll and trying to find another job, the faculty would avoid him and if they couldn't they would be hardy and aggressive

81

and disclaim all responsibility and guiltily smash him on the back. Peggy Bates apologizing with dried chocolate in the corners of her mouth. Grobstein catatonic. Petters with his phoney British superciliousness.

Kincaid rose abruptly from his chair, his plastic plate spinning to the floor. They would be condescending, smug, superior. To him! For such as *they* he had allowed himself to get so worked up? Desperate to be *their* colleague? What a laugh! He grabbed the milk carton and angrily sucked up the last drops. In fact, now that he focused on it, he wouldn't accept tenure if it were offered. A new job would quicken his blood, free his spirit from this paralyzing place. So—thanks a lot but no thanks.

As he walked through the automatic doors, he allowed himself a little skip—thanks but no thanks. He could hardly wait to see the shock register on their faces when he said Why don't you take your piddling little job and . . . He brought his forearm up in the appropriate Italian gesture and finished off by scratching his chin. And don't bother trying to get me to change my mind. It's quite made up.

Goddam, he had forgotten to mention Wisconsin to Harriet.

He walked briskly down the mall. The sun shimmered through a column of water spewing from the fountain. A young man without a shirt practiced rock-climbing ten feet up the golden stones of the church's back wall. Nice. Of course, Wisconsin would be just as nice. But different. All those wonderful dairy farmers. Healthy, red-faced Norwegians. Frozen in half the year and then the long soggy thaw. Mud to your knees. He paused. Did he really want Wisconsin? The rock-climber jumped to the ground and sauntered off.

And would Wisconsin still want him if he were a reject here? In fact, it hadn't exactly been an offer. More like an open-ended inquiry. About whether he would attend MLA. If so, his friend had suggested they have dinner.

He sighed. Another desperate pretense. Whistling past the graveyard. His shoulders collapsed down his arms, and he let his knees sag against the retaining wall around the pool of the fountain. He felt as though he were all exposed nerve and tender flesh. He couldn't face his colleagues just then. Maybe never.

A gray hard-water crust had built up on the tile facing of the fountain wall. Nature protecting the tiles. That's what he needed, a tougher skin. Once his father, trying to persuade him to go to law school, had scoffed that university teaching was The Easy Life. Hohoho to that. Or rather Hunhunhun. Hostile students, judgmental colleagues, ruthless competitors, arrogant administrators—no wonder he was a wreck. To succeed, you had to be a real scholar, like old Cathcart, or devilishly clever, like Petters, who manipulated his career as if he were piloting a 747.

He sat down on the wall. One good thing, if he got fired he could go back to reading literature because he loved it, not just to find something to say in class or write an article on.

He stretched full-length on the wall and closed his eyes against the bright sun. At last the ordeal was grinding to its end. It would soon be over. Thank God for that. He opened one eye and looked at his watch. It was 2:20. They had doubtless finished their cruel deciding and were looking for him to tell him the news.

Abruptly he sat up. He jumped off the wall. Suppose someone found him looking tragic behind the church. He threw back his shoulders, shot his cuffs, ironed down his necktie, and with as springy a walk as he could muster made his way toward his office.

As soon as he turned the corner of the building, he saw a dozen of the faculty lounging in the shadows of the arcade. Every nerve in his body twanged. Every membrane tautened. For a moment he pretended not to see them. But of course that was transparent, and so he glanced up smiling nonchalantly. The first person he saw was somnolent old Grobstein. Grobstein had spread his fingers to form a V. What a dear clever fellow. And then Peggy Bates took a step forward and vigorously thrust her thumbs skyward, a candy bar girlishly caught between her teeth. Darling Peggy.

Cathcart stepped forward and threw his arm across Kincaid's shoulders. "Congratulations, my boy," he said. "One hundred percent in favor of tenure for you. I didn't have to say a word."

Kincaid felt his breath crashing against the lining of his lungs. He was afraid it would explode through his pores. When he let it out, it sounded strangely like the tail-end of a sob. And then all of them converged on him—Ramsay, Petters, even old Casey—and were shaking his hand and pummeling his back and grinning with satisfaction. Grinning, he thought, as though they had done him an immense favor, as though they had achieved a miracle, as though . . . Don't, please don't do that, he pleaded with himself, and answered, I won't, I won't.

"But we mustn't stand here taking your time," said Cathcart. "You'll want to call your lovely Harriet."

"No hurry," said Kincaid. "She's playing tennis."

"I hope the waiting didn't reduce you to jelly," said Petters in his attractive, not-quite-British accent. "They had to scrape me up."

"I broke out in a terrible case of acne," said Cathcart. "Hunhunhun."

And to Thomas Kincaid, the sound of that laugh was music, was the song of larks, was the voice of angels.

Cousins

Margaret had not seen her cousin Robert O'Connor in four years, not since she had left New York to return to the little North Carolina village where she had lived as a child with her grandmother. Robert was a journalist, a bachelor, went everywhere, seemed to know everyone, sheiks and courtesans, athletes and revolutionaries. The image Margaret carried of him was a dapper little man in rather sporty, perhaps checked, traveling clothes, leaning toward her over the railing of an ocean liner, his rueful clown's smile playing hesitantly around his mouth. Now, in answer to her cry for help, he was coming to her, as she knew he would.

"So, big deal," said her son, Phil.

Memories of her and Robert surfaced. Hers had been a lonely childhood, protected and friendless. During the winters she had only her grandmother—a grande dame from Atlanta turned recluse in the resort village—and the silent mountain women who did the cooking and the cleaning. In the summers, she had Robert. They were two lonely children and fast, best friends. She remembered the summer they had broken the glass to enter a deserted mountain cabin, and he had bandaged her cut fingers with old Kleenex. She remembered the summer she was thirteen and he fifteen, and they had kissed a lot, practicing, they told each other, for when it was time to kiss real people. Another summer, lying on the grassy bank of the creek, staring down into her shimmering reflection in the water while Robert read aloud from Hopkins ("Margaret, are you grieving / Over Goldengrove unleaving?"). And the look of sadness on his face the night they met at the top of Chicken Head Rock, her favorite place, for her to

85

tell him she would not marry him. She was eighteen then, and she said she wanted to be only for herself. "I," she declared, "am my own garden." And he said, "You consign me to being no one's."

It was true that she had intended never to marry. But during her last year at Sweetbriar, she discovered that all her friends who had said they would never marry were busy planning elaborate weddings. The young man she chose was desired by many other young women; he told her that he accepted, even admired, what he called her self-possession; he promised to take her to live in New York. All of this struck her as a good basis for love. But after a short time she knew she did not love him, that perhaps she would never love. She said to Robert, as they lunched together during one of his trips back to New York, "The trouble with marriage is that one is expected to *be* with the other, evenings, weekends, holidays." And they both laughed.

Before she had time to separate herself from her husband, she found that she was pregnant. When her son Philip was born—a fragile, absurd creature, a caricature of herself, fair as she was, his eyes slightly upturned as hers were—she was shocked by the tenderness she felt. He became the inescapable fact of her life. After five more years of her "self-possession," her husband became something of a brute, and so she asked Robert to find her a Mexican lawyer.

Afterward, she became a copy editor at one of New York's most elegant women's stores. Men from the store, manufacturers, husbands of women she lunched with crept from her apartment, puzzled by her availability, her remoteness. Strangers she met at parties, in bars, felt resentful as they tied their shoes and went out into the dawn. That was their lookout.

Her lookout was her son. At two o'clock one morning, she heard him weeping. He was ten, puritanical, jealous, lonely. Her grandmother had left the ramshackle old house to her and Robert, and so she cabled Robert (whose most recent postmark said Madrid) that she would like to live in the house if he agreed. He had cabled back, "What you want has always been what I want."

Margaret went off, son in hand, to build a new life in the quiet village where her old self lay hidden, waiting to be discovered. She found that she did quite well, better even, without men, friends, noise, entertainment. She preferred the old house, resonant with memories, the neglected garden where she had often sat gazing at the sky, the rich moist comforting foliage along the creek, the hot hard rocks above, the clear reflecting water below.

Of course, she still had her son. Oh, how she had him. For the first years of their exile, they were the best of friends. They played together (tennis, Scrabble), did puzzles together (a thousand pieces of blue sky), and read together (Dickens, Tolkien, Carroll). Phil's victory over his nameless rivals had left him complacent and malleable.

The smallest worm will turn, being trodden upon. Not that she thought she trod, but turn he did, as the treacherous storm of his teens blew up around them. Phil at fifteen no longer resembled her. He was six feet tall, a beautiful rebel with melting brown eyes, dark hair that curled around his ears, and a cold sneer. He had been known to pick his toenails at the kitchen table, eyeing her malevolently. Boys with darting hillbilly eyes sat in her living room (all day, it seemed, all night) marking time as a rock band shrieked accompaniment. Phil boasted that he had smoked marijuana, snorted coke. He had often stolen her car for races over mountain roads. When she spoke to him, he seemed to grow immense, bristling and swelling like a cat's tail. While she had slept, a monster had invaded her life.

Little wonder she had asked for help from the only human being who would gladly give it. Of course he would come, he wired—he would arrive on the tenth of June.

She spent a half hour selecting a shirt to go with her jeans, brushing her hair until it glowed, choosing between sneakers and sandals, deciding on sandals to show that at least the dregs of her femininity remained. She begged Phil to accompany her to the little train depot. He went, but he went as he was, shirtless, his cut-offs hanging from his hip bones. As the train labored to a halt, they stood together, Margaret with her shyly smiling face lifted to the passing windows; Phil with his perfect white teeth angrily covered and his perfect belly button exposed like a third eye that never blinked.

Robert stepped down from the train and started forward, frowning and smiling, mocking and abiding the custom of greetings. He was dressed in a dark blazer and a bright red-striped shirt and gray trousers. An elegant man with a funny face, with the nose of a small hawk and ears like half-saucers stuck in his head. Margaret wanted to say to Phil, But notice the intelligent eyes and the sensitive, humorous mouth.

Margaret and Robert embraced and kissed. Robert turned to Phil, his tentative smile declaring that he longed to be liked, that he hoped to connect. After a reluctant handshake and without speaking, Phil picked up the scarred suitcase with its dozens of customs stickers and led the way back to the car. Robert sat in the passenger seat beside Margaret. When they stopped at the village's only stoplight, they heard a ripping sound from the back seat. They turned to see Phil balling up a decal torn from the suitcase. Phil flushed as they turned.

"Tear them all off," said Robert. "They make me look like a boarding school girl home from the Grand Tour."

Phil tore off a few more. In a grudging tone, he asked, "What do you do? I mean, that you get to travel all over."

"I'm a free-lance journalist," said Robert. "No special assignment, just what's happening, current trends. What kind of bathing suits the Beautiful People are sporting at what toney resort in what newly discovered country. What the Yugoslavs or the Iraqi are doing about birth control or VD. That sort of thing."

Phil snorted and said, "Bullshit."

Without a pause, Robert said, "Yeah, but top-grade, 4-H Club-quality bulls only." Phil snorted again, and then allowed a laugh to escape his lips.

"That's pretty good," he said. "4-H Club bulls."

During the first two days of the visit, Phil hung on the edges of their conversation, sat a little longer over meals, stopped briefly outside open doorways to listen, occasionally shot Robert quick questions ("Did you ever see the Loch Ness Monster?") though hardly waited for an answer (Robert called after him, "No, but the girl I saw was mighty ugly"), and then came back (to say, "That's pretty good"). Robert's presence seemed to confer upon the house a lightness and serenity it had not known for a long time. Margaret began to relax.

By the third day, Phil was content to stay at home with them, to make a third. He took on the responsibility of entertaining Robert. The two played tennis together. They fished for trout in the cold mountain stream where Margaret and Robert had waded as children. They prepared the catch for dinner.

"Shall I fry up the guts for the local cats?" asked Phil. He held a mass of slime and laughing at Margaret let it plop into the sink. He turned to leave the room.

Robert took him by the shoulder and guided him back to the sink. "You are the garbage man," he said. After that, Phil carried out the garbage without being told.

Phil stayed around throughout the afternoon. When his friends came by, he spoke to them through the windows of their ancient cars and waved them on. In the evening, the three of them played a boisterous game of Hearts and then sat on the verandah while Robert speculated aloud on the sex lives of neighbors who walked out for the evening cool, and Phil howled with laughter.

On the fourth day, Phil and Robert drove the thirty-five miles over the mountains to Asheville to shop for fruits and delicacies. Phil brought Margaret a large ripe Persian melon and held it out to her as if he had created it.

"He brings you a melon," said Robert, "but I know your true secret passion." He presented her with ten Hershey bars with almonds. "In the old days," he said to Phil, "I would be mad with longing while she sat contentedly munching chocolate bars."

Amidst the laughter, Phil said, "Hey, I'm the one who loves candy now, you know." He grabbed for the bars.

89

Robert said, "No. At your age, you'd get pimples."

"That's not much fun," said Phil.

"Fun?" said Robert scornfully. "Civilization flourishes when fun is abandoned."

"Forget you," said Phil.

"All right," said Robert. "Not abandoned—postponed, delayed for more pleasure later." He winked at Margaret. "You want chocolate, you eat chocolate, you have pleasure, and you have pimples. Right? How about this: you want chocolate, but you don't eat chocolate because you have wisely been instructed not to, and you therefore have this great complexion." He flicked Phil's cheek. "Now this: you meet a nice little mountain wench who's just mad for your great complexion and voila! you're in the hayloft. Take your pick."

Margaret said, "Oh, let him have the chocolate."

"I prefer the hayloft," said Phil. Margaret watched as his fantasy played with the girl in the hayloft. His smile was reckless and delicious. Rather than a petulant, overbearing child, he was a beautiful young man. Robert had wrought a miracle.

The next morning before Robert was up, Phil came into the kitchen where Margaret sat. He put his hand on her neck. "I have a declaration," he said. "I want to say that I'm truly sorry about the last year. I've been such a . . . I guess I shouldn't say son of a bitch, should I?" They laughed at that, and he went on. "Robert keeps saying I don't appreciate you enough, that you're one hell of a woman. He says you've given up a lot for me."

"Oh, he did, did he? And what did he say I'd given up?"

"He didn't exactly say, but I figure it must have been Robert." His grin was self-consciously ironic, pleased at his wit. "I wouldn't mind, you know, if I'm what's holding you back." He frowned and became boyishly serious. "You have to think about the future. I won't be around forever, you know. What'll happen to you then?"

"Perhaps I'd like it," she answered. "One lamb chop, one artichoke. I could be utterly self-centered then. I wouldn't have to think of anyone but me."

90

"Robert is one hell of a guy," Phil assured her.

That day without explanation Robert extended his visit beyond the promised six days. Phil was obviously delighted. He and Robert did odd paint jobs, replaced rotten window sills, pruned the elm trees, and bound the cuttings for kindling.

"Don't you want to see what we've accomplished?" called Phil.

"A little later," she answered from behind the drawn blinds of her room. "I'll inspect it all a little later." She had taken to spending more and more time in her room, lying on her bed, reading, day-dreaming, quite content to hear the murmur of their talk from a distant corner of the house.

Robert's attitude toward her was affectionate and ironic. When they sat on the verandah in the loveseat swing, while Phil on the steps below meticulously explained himself and the world, Robert held her hand and idly played with her fingers. When they went to their rooms, he kissed her cheek.

She was grateful that he did not insist beyond these shows of affection. For she could not bring herself to think of him as a lover. She told herself that they had known each other too long, Robert had no mystery, no otherness for her. There was the old pattern of acceptance of each other, cousins, from long ago when she had been willing to roam the mountain for long evenings with him because he understood and did not claw her as the other boys did. And she did not wish now to be aroused, disturbed, to begin all that again, to be touched and grasped, to be imprisoned in someone else's urgency, or in her own.

Yet she saw that his presence alleviated many problems and took the burden of Phil off her. She imagined the future when he left—herself and Phil in the kitchen amidst the drying egg yolk, the moist, mouthed crusts of toast, Phil's face roughened by rage, his vibrant voice assaulting her, penetrating her being. She thought that Robert protected her from this vision. If only they could stay forever like this.

Robert seemed to understand how she felt and did not force himself on her. Sometimes she turned and caught him staring

91

at her, a gaze she felt was half-expectant, half-sorrowful. But always he smiled quickly as if to relieve her of the pressure of his disappointment, to assure her that the time with her was all he asked. And he would lift her hand and lightly kiss her fingertips. Often he treated her as if she were a delicate invalid or a highly prized guest.

"It's my house, too, you know," he said. "Pretend you're a lady, pretend I'm a gentleman. Let me take care of you. I have a lovely idea. Tonight a picnic of everything expensive and rare. Let me take care of everything. I can, you know."

He and Phil went off again to shop in Asheville and returned loaded with delicacies—caviar, endive, raspberries, sausages, Camembert, two bottles of Moselle. Robert said, "We're going to start civilizing this great beast of yours, make his manners fit for the finest spas. Refrigerate the wine, let the Camembert breathe. Two of the Ten Commandments." He smiled at Margaret.

"What are the other eight?" asked Phil.

Robert pretended outrage. "Even God took seven days, and he didn't have such recalcitrant material. This creation will take time."

"I'm afraid you won't be around long enough to finish the job," said Margaret.

"Don't be too sure, just don't be too sure," he answered.

In early evening they spread an old army blanket over the top of Chicken Head Rock and unloaded the picnic hamper. Margaret made a sandwich of sausages and Camembert and French bread and poured herself a glass of wine.

"Did you see that?" cried Robert, pointing into the woods along the bank. "I swear it was a fox."

"Baloney," said Phil. "There aren't any foxes in this area."

"A bet," said Robert. "We'll track it and then I want your profuse apology and one dollar." They ran off into the woods.

Margaret lay across the blanket, her chin braced on the beak of the chicken. The heat of the sun flowed from the rock into her body. She stared at the water as a silvery shadow shimmered across the reflection of her face and then disappeared among the rocks of the creekbed. She brushed a pebble into the water and watched as her reflection quivered. She watched her smile re-form.

She closed her eyes when she heard their good-humored quarreling coming closer and closer. There had been fox traces; not. Droppings: only rabbits.

She felt their presence, their nearness, and she opened her eyes, staring into the water. They were leaning out over her, to see what she saw, and in the water she saw their reflections, more distant, vaguer than hers, blocking out the sky. She wished they had stayed away a little longer, not brought their insistent sounds back to her.

"What are you looking at?" Phil asked.

"Trout?" asked Robert. "Phil, you idiot, you should have brought the fishing tackle."

"Me? *You* should have."

"Oh, do hush," she said. She twisted onto her back. "If there were a trout or foxes or human beings or any creature, your clamor would drive them away." She lifted her hands to be pulled up. "Help me."

Robert laughed and pulled her to her feet. "I love you," he said, dropping his wrists on her shoulders, "which hasn't been news in nearly twenty-five years. Do you really appreciate what a wonder she is?" he asked Phil. "How remote, how unobtainable, how she ruined all other women for me, how I cannot get out of her clutches or . . . or into her bed? How I've panted longingly after her since I first wore long pants?" Robert peered at her closely. She felt herself recoil, but she did not move away.

"Break it up, you two," said Phil, "or better yet make it legal." He cocked his head with delight.

That night her dreams were anxious and feverish. She felt her body tenderly stroked. She felt the ache in her groin, the tensing of her thighs. She opened her eyes to the first light of day, to the cheep of birds. Outside her window on a limb of an elm tree, birds sang and birds copulated. The male bird mounted, fluttered furiously for a brief moment, flew off. She heard the shrill whine of a cat. She heard a dog bark as though with longing. All of nature seemed to be mating, to be coming together.

She slipped on a robe and moved silently down the hall to Robert's room. She stood beside his bed and looked at him. Dear, vulnerable, funny-looking Robert. He wanted only what she wanted. He had said that, more than once. But what was it, what did she want?

Robert rolled onto his back and opened his eyes. He held his hand toward her and when she took it he pulled her down to sit on the edge of the bed. He stroked her hand. She wanted to overcome her aversion, to open herself to him. Had she then become a virgin again, fearful, protecting herself against invasion? Not yet, she thought, not now. She stood up and pulled her robe tighter around her body. As she walked to her room, she heard the sibilant peeling away of her bare feet from the wooden floor.

After lunch the next day, Robert suggested that they sit on the verandah to catch the brief freshening breeze that early each afternoon blew from the mountain. Phil sat in the love-seat swing, his arms spread across the back in a lordly gesture of ownership. Robert and Margaret faced each other in the weather-beaten wicker rockers. They rocked and swung in silence for a moment or two. Robert, she thought, looked purposive, tense, his wide humorous mouth drawn down.

As she waited for him to speak, she felt a dull ache begin at the base of her skull. She had lived alone so long, hidden away in the little village, the passages to her inner being closed to all save Phil. Naturally, she assured herself, she would be uneasy, fearful, now that Robert was forcing those passages. Finally, he spoke.

"I have to admit I wasn't exactly eager to come down here. I didn't know what you really wanted of me, Margaret, and your recent letters made Phil sound so awful. But I've always cared about you, a lot. You were the image I always carried, the unobtainable, the ideal woman. So when you asked for help, I decided I'd answer. So—here I am. What do you think, don't you agree we've got on awfully well?"

94

"We've got on famously," said Margaret. She held herself tense, ready for what he had to say.

"*We* always did," he said. "I meant, me and Phil. Well, Phil, why don't I just say it?"

"For Pete's sake, yeah," said Phil, thrashing about on the swing.

"I've got to be in London three days from now," said Robert. "I was wondering if Phil might come and be my guest for the rest of the summer." He looked at her quizzically.

She did not respond at once. No one seemed to be breathing. There was no breeze at all. She felt the dampness of sweat between her breasts. She closed her eyes against the image of herself and opened them to look at Robert. He seemed to back off, to shy away from her scrutiny. She let her gaze wander to the silken nervous fingers pinching along the crease of his trousers. He did not want her after all. She sighed. She smiled. She was safe.

"Well, what do you think, Margaret?"

"He wouldn't want to go," she said. "His friends mean too much," she explained. "He's a regular hillbilly himself. Imagine Phil in where? Those toney places you go? And anyway what about that mountain wench after all?" She teased Phil with a smile.

"Not want to go to Europe?" he said incredulously. "Not want to travel with Robert?" He eyed her through lowered lids. "Maybe you think I adore being here with you."

She heard the whish and creak of the swing as Phil pressed his angry thighs into the seat. She peered at him, saw the twist of petulance on his lower lip, the threatening droop of his eyes.

"He'd be a nuisance," she said. "You don't know what a pain he can be." With her words, Phil seemed to swell up, immense with his anger.

Robert said, "Oh, if that's all. I'd take a leather strop to him if he acts up, as I believe he thinks he's about to do now." He leaned forward and playfully cuffed Phil on the side of the head. Grudgingly Phil smiled, and tense breath burst from him. "I have untapped reserves of fatherly sternness and discipline," Robert went on. "I'm what he needs." He paused and smiled at her, a familiar look, ironic, sorrowful, false. "This lummox of yours will be my chance to show you how much I could have meant to you. If you had only let me."

"Already, God, look what he's done," said Phil. He held his clean hands toward her and rubbed his thumbs across the neatly trimmed fingernails.

"Wonders," said Margaret. They seemed to accept that as a sign of consent. They murmured with satisfaction.

"We've got it figured out," said Robert. "There's a plane out of Asheville for New York at noon tomorrow. Then fly to London next day."

"London," said Phil. He and Robert smiled at each other. They looked foolish and a little abashed and self-important.

"And I would be alone," she said. "Alone." For an instant the word seemed to take wing and she with it. All the blue sky.

"One artichoke, one lamb chop," Phil reminded her.

Robert brought his rocker up onto the points of the runners and leaned close to her. "I suspect you'd like that a great deal," he said in a high, pressing voice, "while your two men wander around the world together." He smiled a coaxing smile. "Yesterday when we nearly caught that fox—yes, it was a fox, Phil, be quiet—you as much as told us you were tired of us. I imagine you'd like being alone for a change."

"Perhaps you're right," she said. Her voice, coming back to her off his pleased expression, sounded as though she believed him. Perhaps she did. She imagined herself alone on Chicken Head Rock, peering down into the water at her reflection against the blue sky, surrounded by only the blue-white sky. Her true self lay hidden in that reflection. It would take a lifetime to understand it, to rediscover it. And now she would be free of those who grasped her, lovers and friends and family, free of Robert, free of Phil.

"Yes," she said, "it's what I want. You want what I want."

Robert sighed and let the rocker fall back. "She's wonderful, isn't she, Phil? There's never been any woman quite like her."

She heard the dry scraping of the wind as it twisted through the evergreens. At last the breeze was coming up. She felt the cold move along her arms, slide inside the loose sleeves of her dress, caress her body. When it crept to the soft hairs of her neck, she shivered. She stood up. She wouldn't look at Phil. It was better, really, for both of them. All of them. She looked at Robert.

"I'd better see to his clothes," she said. "We wouldn't want him looking shabby, would we?" She moved with a light step toward the door.

Making Amends

The woman parked the car at the curb just beyond the restaurant. A misty rain, little more than fog, had begun to fall, and she ran the few steps to the shelter of the marquee. She unlatched her handbag, dropped in her car keys, and looked at herself in the storefront windows that had been painted a reflecting black. She was in her forties, slender, blond, and carefully tended. She smoothed the hair along her temples, pulled the collar of her coat a little closer around her throat, dried the corners of her mouth with her thumb and forefinger, and then opened the restaurant door.

The restaurant was small and dark. On each of the dozen tables a candle flickered in a frosted globe. When the woman appeared in the little glassed-in vestibule, the man at the corner table stood up. He was perhaps a few years older than the woman, certainly more worn. His face was deeply creased and shadowed, and his hair had faded to a dull pale copper. He raised his hand to his shoulder in a half-gesture of greeting and waited for her to acknowledge him. When she looked at him and smiled, he called "Ellen" and immediately started toward her. The other diners glanced up, apparently saw nothing particularly arresting about these two middle-aged people, and turned back to their cream sauces and wine and talk.

As the man approached, the woman held out her hand, palm down. "How nice," she said in a soft modulated voice, "how glad I am to see you after, my God, Gordon, I don't know how many years."

The man took her hand and said, "Please be gladder than that." He hesitated a moment and then leaned forward as though to kiss her, but she had turned to the proprietor.

The proprietor led them to the corner table. "May I take your coat?" he asked.

"It's a little cold in here," said Ellen. "I'll keep it."

The proprietor held her chair, and she sat down. She drew her arms from the coat sleeves and then pulled the coat up over her shoulders like a cape.

"You always did that," Gordon said, nodding. He placed himself at a right angle to her. "Got in and out of your coat sitting down. Neat trick. I always thought you kept your coat as a kind of protection." He watched her face.

"Perhaps I did, and perhaps I do," she said after a pause. "Or perhaps I'm just a little cold-blooded."

"I certainly never thought of you as cold-blooded," he said. She didn't respond. He sat back in his chair, appraising her, a look of wonderment growing on his face. "You're lovely, just lovely," he said. "Better even. You've gotten even better with the years." He paused. "Most wines, some cheeses, but very, very few women."

She glanced at him, unsmiling, and then around the room at the other diners. "I'm always surprised when there's no one I know. San Francisco isn't really that big." She drew the napkin from the wine glass and shook it out across her lap.

"I'm sorry," said Gordon. "That was the kind of dumb remark I've learned to make without even thinking. I should have known I couldn't get away with anything like that with you. Never could." He sighed. "But I do mean it—just lovely."

"Thank you," she said. She looked at him. "What brings you to town?"

"I told you when I called from L.A. I came solely to see you. If you hadn't been able, or willing, to see me, I wouldn't have come."

"I've always been here, more or less."

"I know, and frankly it's been difficult to avoid the Bay Area all these years, but I managed. You know, I haven't been back to Berkeley since the day I graduated."

"So why now?" she asked. It was hardly a question.

Gordon motioned to the waiter and the waiter started across

the room. "What would you say if I said I wanted a new start in life and I thought I could maybe get it if I went back to where it had gone wrong?"

"I'd say you were a hopeless romantic," Ellen answered.

He leaned toward her. "But wasn't I always?" The waiter stood patiently beside the table. "In my fashion? Wanting everything? Never satisfied? Wasn't that my downfall?"

Ellen said, "I didn't know you had a downfall. I'll have a martini," she said to waiter. "Straight up. Icy cold."

Gordon said, "Perrier, with lime." When the waiter left, Gordon rested his elbow on the table and his chin on the heel of his palm. He gazed at her quizzically. "And you? Are you still a romantic?"

"Was I ever?"

He drew back. "The great artist? Willing to live in an attic on a crust of bread? Our generation's Mary Cassatt?"

She laughed. "Imagine remembering that."

"I remember everything," he said somberly. "Everything about those days."

"Then you'll remember," she said in a voice gone suddenly harsh, "that I didn't go to Paris to study after all." She forced a little laugh. "I'm quite content now just to buy and sell. I realized I wasn't meant to be an artist. I suppose that's when I stopped being a romantic."

"So much the worse for me," he said. "Romantics are more malleable, more forgiving."

"Oh, I'm much more forgiving, though perhaps not quite so malleable."

Now they looked at each other without speaking, but smiling politely. Finally Gordon said, "Whatever you've become inside, you've gotten downright elegant outside." His eyes took her in, the well-cut hair, the sapphire earrings, the bracelet glittering on the cuff of her dark silk dress, her shapely hands resting lightly on the edge of the table. "I really didn't expect you to be quite as chic as you are."

"Was I so dowdy?" she asked, laughing. "So unkempt as all that?"

"I would have said above such matters," he answered. "That

was your brand of romanticism, rejecting the superficialities of life." He plucked the lapel of his gray jacket. "I still can't wear a blue blazer without feeling either wicked or trite, like one of the fraternity boys you despised. You almost made a revolutionary out of me, or at least a monk."

"Did I? I didn't know I had such influence."

"Perhaps more than you know," he said. "You were so pure, so uncorruptible."

She dismissed that with a shrug. "One does grow up."

He smiled. "And some do it beautifully."

"I had Edward's help. That made all the difference."

Gordon nodded. He touched the sapphire bracelet. "He must have been what? successful at least? maybe important?"

"At least and maybe," she said.

"I'd say life's been pretty damn good to you. You can tell when a woman's been loved and taken care of. Truly loved and taken care of."

"Yes," she said, "I've been loved and taken care of."

He thought for a moment. "But no one does it now?" he asked.

"I do it now," she said. "I take care of myself. I run the gallery now. I do it very well. I have a very good, full life."

"But alone?" he persisted. "No one special in it?"

They watched each other. Finally she said, "After Edward's death, there were some. But I don't make connections easily, and anyway none could possibly measure up, so why bother. I prefer my life the way it is. I go where I please when I please with whom I please. I do exactly as I please."

"And no regrets? No lonely moments?"

She glanced toward the open doorway where the proprietor stood smoking, blowing smoke out into the rainy night. "I'm afraid we haven't been very nice to you with the weather," she said, turning back. "You'd probably forgotten how some winters it rained and rained and rained. Yes, there are lonely moments. I won't pretend there aren't." She paused. "And then I start a new novel, plan a trip, put different music on the record player."

"Ah," he said, "Haydn instead of Liszt."

101

"Or the Beatles instead of Billie Holiday. And the mood passes."

"Still sometimes you must hope . . ."

"As I said, I'm not a romantic. And you? Have you been loved and taken care of?"

He threw up his hands and laughed. "By dozens and dozens. My irresistible charm, you know."

"Alas, I do," she said. "Or rather I did."

He let out a comic sigh. "That's the trouble in a nutshell— lots of did and no do these days." He touched his knife and it rang softly against his spoon. "I have to admit that all my vaunted charm has added up to very little. Now I have nothing."

As soon as the words were spoken, he grimaced and brushed the air with his hand as though to wipe away the words. "I shouldn't have said that. Sounds so awfully abject, doesn't it?" He looked at her in mock exasperation. "You always did that, made me honest in spite of myself even when it hurt." He nodded. "Yes, now I have nothing and no one."

She put her hand on his sleeve. "I'm awfully sorry things didn't work out for you."

He looked at her hand for a moment and then jerked his arm away as if stung. "Oh, come on now. You're really not one bit sorry, except in some conventional, moralistic way, which isn't like you even if you have grown up. Actually, you're glad. Serves me right, right? to have made a botch of my life while yours has been happiness itself. Except, of course, you didn't plan on being alone the last half." He looked thoughtful. Hitching his chair a little closer to her, he said, "When you think about it, our situations aren't all that different now, are they? We've both ended up alone."

She admonished him with a raised finger. "Except I am really quite content the way I am and you are obviously . . . abject, didn't you call it?"

He groaned, winced, laughed. "There you go, being honest. I still find it hard to take."

The waiter set the martini in front of Ellen and a small Perrier and a glass of ice with a slice of lime on the rim in front of Gordon. He gave each a leather folder and for a few minutes they sipped their drinks and studied the menu.

Without looking up, Ellen said, "You might have written. That was what I minded most—the sudden silence after all the letters, after . . . everything."

Gordon glanced up and quickly back down. After a moment, he said, "I kept thinking I would, tomorrow, next week, next month, explaining, telling you everything. I guess I just took the easy way out and let it slide into oblivion." Ellen said nothing, and he went on. "As it turns out, it wasn't the easy way at all. Here I am, twenty-odd years later, trying to make amends."

"Twenty-three," she said without looking up. "The lamb looks good, but I think I'll have the tournedos."

He seized on that. "Well done, right? Gray all the way through to the bone? Cooked to death?" He laughed. "I kept telling you it was not sophisticated to eat meat well done, but you were stubborn to the end. You see I have not forgotten one thing about you, one moment we were together."

She closed the folder. Her smile was a challenge. "I bet I remember more. Loser pays for dinner?"

"You're on. What was showing at the opera the night my uncle gave us the tickets?"

She thought a moment. "My slip?"

He looked delighted and made a little check in the air. "Yours. Here's another: what was the name of the inn we stayed at in Mendocino the weekend your mother caught you in the lie?"

Color flushed through her cheeks, but she smiled distantly. "My mind's a blank. I always repress my lies."

"I may forgive you that little lapse," he said frowning and shaking his head, "if you remember the name of our first hotel. Or have you forgotten that, too?"

She held his gaze. "The Pine Inn in Carmel."

They looked steadily at each other, not smiling. He leaned closer to her and almost whispered. "That was one of the best things in my life, having you love and trust me that much. And I was nice, wasn't I? Wasn't I what I should have been for you?"

"Yes," she said, "you were very nice." She glanced around the room and barely nodded to the waiter.

Gordon leaned back in his chair. "I don't think I could have stood it if you hadn't said that."

The waiter stood beside the table with his pencil poised. "I'll start with the artichoke vinaigrette and then the tournedos," Ellen said. She shot a look at Gordon. "Rare. Very, very rare." Laughing lightly, she drew her shoulders forward and flung her coat over the back of the chair.

Gordon's shout of laughter rang out. "Wonderful. Wonderful," he said. "I do get the message. I'll have the same, except make my steak just plain rare." They both laughed.

When the waiter offered the wine list, Gordon said, "I won't, but will you?"

The waiter said, "If you'd like just a glass, the house red is a nice Beaujolais." Ellen nodded and the waiter left.

"Perrier? No wine?" Ellen asked.

"I assumed you understood." He pulled at the puckers under his eyes. "I'm an ex-lush. Very lush but very, very ex. I think." He smiled ruefully. "The trouble is, I'm more charming when I'm slightly boozy."

"You're doing all right sober," Ellen said.

He straightened and took a deep breath. "That little comment will probably extend my sobriety by a good six months."

"And after that?"

He looked at her a long moment. "Enough such could last me all my days."

"Was that your downfall, as you put it?"

"Not really," he said. "A symptom, not the cause. The cause was . . . what shall I say? Recognition of my inadequacy? I date the downfall from that summer I went to France. Remember how I wanted to be a serious scholar and learn to read literature in the French way?"

"I had thought that was why you went. At least so you said."

He didn't pick up on her tone. "The first six months I hung

104

around the cafés with my mouth open, utterly astonished by the other students."

"You said the women were all hirsute and the men carried dynamite in their pockets."

He shook his head as though still puzzled. "They were so smart, so learned, so serious. I was way out of my depth."

"You didn't write that," she said.

"I couldn't stand your disapproval, your disappointment. You expected too much of me. Always had. Anyway, it wasn't long before I realized I was better suited for the Champs Elysées, Maxim's, that sort of thing. So I gradually moved my base of operations over there."

"Maxim's? A struggling student? Living on a shoestring?"

He shrugged. "If you're fairly amusing and accessible, it's not too difficult. Still, I would have stuck it if you'd been with me." He moaned. "I really needed you that winter."

Her response was quick and sharp, and delivering it she leaned toward him, almost over him. "What for? Couldn't you find someone else to worship you? Follow you around like a puppy dog? Go to class and take notes and write papers so you could be charming on the Champs Elysées? Is that why you needed me?" She pushed back her chair, unlatched her handbag, and took out her car keys. She waited, poised as though to leave.

He wouldn't look at her. "We don't remember it quite the same way, apparently," he said. "I needed you because you made me better than I was. I needed you so we could be warm and good and loving with each other as we had been, both of us. You weren't my puppy dog. Try to be fair to me, please." Now he looked at her. "I didn't use you. I loved you."

"I guess my memory isn't very good," she shot back. "I had quite forgotten that." But she dropped her keys back in her bag and relatched it. She lifted the martini to her lips and watched him over the rim of the glass. For all his ruined cragginess, his face was boyishly resentful. At last she said, "Not fair. I do remember." Now he glanced up at her and quickly said,

"Okay, here's another: what was the name of the fancy restaurant I took you to on your twenty-first birthday?"

She puzzled. "Fancy restaurant? I don't remember that you ever took me to a fancy restaurant."

"That cost me two weeks' allowance, and you don't even remember?"

"It must have been some other girl."

"What other girl could it have been? *You* were my girl. Even though you seem to have forgotten it."

She laughed. "You never took me anywhere but the student union and that pizza joint on Shattuck Avenue."

"Ingrate! Liar! False friend!" he almost shouted, throwing himself back in his chair. "And I suppose you don't remember that gorgeous paisley scarf I did without lunch for a whole week to buy you or the complete Proust that first Christmas?"

"Oh, I remember the Proust all right," she said. "Of course, I couldn't read a word of French and you borrowed it within the week. Don't you think it's time you returned it?"

Laughing he said, "Was it my fault you were so ignorant, so untutored? God knows I tried to educate you."

"Ignorant? Who explained Jackson Pollock to whom? Who explained cubism? Who explained color field to the color blind?"

"Who helped whom to pass physics? Who . . ."

Through the artichokes, the tournedos, her wine, his second Perrier, the coffee, they talked and teased about the past. Sometimes they choked with laughter, sometimes they grew somber. The conversation moved across the intervening years. She told him about Edward, the years they knew each other before she would marry him, their daughter, their son, both now in school in the East, and then Edward's accident on a winding Swiss road. He told her about his three wives, the first married—he lowered his eyes to tell it—two years after he went to Paris. That wife was a Swede, a beautiful Valkyrie, he said, with a huge hunk of Volvo stock and a generous spirit when they were divorced. The second was Italian with an ancient name and vineyards. He had not seen his two daughters

106

in nearly three years. His third wife was merely American, merely rich.

"Her farewell present," he said, "was six weeks at a health spa in Baja California. Before she cast me overboard, she wanted to be sure I could swim." He waited, but Ellen only listened. "Afterwards, when I got in the car she left me, I thought, Okay, I can drive east to Phoenix and spend a week with an old friend and then on to, oh, maybe Oklahoma City for a weekend with a cousin and . . . and so on. Or I can drive south into Mexico, scene of mistakes itching to be remade. Of course, I could have driven due west, but I wasn't ready for that. So—I drove due north."

"To San Francisco, to Berkeley, after all this time."

"To you," he said. "No more avoiding. Once I thought of seeing you, it just seemed absolutely right and necessary." He lifted one of her hands from her lap and held it under his on the surface of the table. "What I did to you left something festering in me, a permanent wound that I inflicted not only on you but also on myself. I thought if I could just see you, acknowledge what had happened, make it up to you somehow . . ." He shook his head. "I really am a hopeless romantic. You've probably hated me all these years."

"There was a time," she said quietly, "when I ached for revenge."

"And didn't you get it?" he said. "Wasn't the real revenge being happy, living well, all that? The awful irony is that the whole thing seems to have done you a world of good." He looked at her keenly, and an expression of admiring disbelief settled on his face. "Do you get down on your knees every night and thank God you didn't marry me?"

"Only on weeknights and every other Sunday."

Her hand was still under his and he rubbed his thumb along her fingers. After a moment, he said, "Would you tell me what went on in your mind when you heard my voice after all these years?"

She slipped her hand free and picked up her coffee cup though it was empty. "What I saw," she said, "was the beau-

107

tiful young man with the glowing dark eyes who could always make me laugh." She pressed the cup against her lips and then carefully, soundlessly, returned it to the saucer. "And what I felt was the abiding humiliation." With a faint smile on her face, she watched him.

He closed his eyes, and they sat in silence. He wagged his head back and forth, back and forth. Finally he opened his eyes. "May I ask what you're thinking now?"

They were the last diners. At the front table, the waiter was drinking wine with the proprietor and the cook. Ellen said, "They're waiting. We should let them go home." Gordon turned and nodded to the waiter. "You were my great romance," Ellen said. "I don't deny that. I haven't forgotten that."

An enormous glad smile broke across Gordon's face, and he touched her cheek with his fingertips, very delicately.

The waiter set the tray on the corner of the table. Ellen quickly reached for it, saying, "I think you won the bet. I didn't remember the opera or the fancy restaurant and a lot of other things."

Gordon caught her wrist and placed her hand in her lap. "I get a very healthy dividend from Volvo every quarter. I am far from destitute." He took out his wallet and extracted some bills. "God, what you must think of me." He put the bills on the tray, stood up, braced himself with his fists on the table, and leaned over. "Let's get one thing straight. I didn't come here to see if you were rich—the world is full of rich. Palm Springs and Palm Beach and Palm This and Palm That are just jumping with rich, eager widows. That's easy, believe me." He ducked his head to see into her eyes. "The reason I came is the reason I told you—I want to try to pick up my life where it went wrong. I hope you'll help."

Ellen reached behind her and slipped her arms into the sleeves of her coat. She drew the collar around her neck.

Gordon straightened. "Ah, now you're back in your armor."

Her smile was shy. "I'm beginning to think I may need it."

The rain was coming down hard when they went outside. They stopped under the marquee. Gordon put his hands on Ellen's shoulders and turned her to face him. He brushed the hair from her forehead. "I'm parked a couple of blocks away," he said in a husky voice. "Will you let me take you home?"

Ellen glanced up and down the street. She looked at the car parked at the curb just beyond the restaurant. She turned back to Gordon. "All right," she said.

He pulled her to him and held her. "Five minutes," he whispered, and stepped out into the rain.

Ellen watched him jog down the street. The wind rose a bit and carried the rain under the awning, and Ellen shielded herself in the doorway of the restaurant. The door was propped open with a chair and inside the waiter was folding a pink napkin into the shape of a rose. Carefully he placed the napkin in the wine glass. A minute passed. The street was silent except for the sibilance of tires over wet pavement in the distance and the chink of rain on the canvas above her. Ellen opened her handbag, took out her car keys, and ran through the rain to her car.

Just as she drove away, a car turned into the street. It stopped in front of the restaurant, and Gordon got out. He stood on the sidewalk under the marquee, waiting, jangling the coins in his pocket, looking up and down the empty street.

Ellen climbed the carpeted staircase to her bedroom. She placed her earrings and bracelet in a velvet-lined case. She hung up her dress and put on a fresh lavender nightgown and dressing gown. She switched on the bedside radio. Music swelled into the room. She sat on the edge of the bed, listening to the music, swaying a little to the rhythm. Then with a swift motion, she turned the dial to another station.

Saturday People

Stancy noticed them first, of course. "Look, Mom, she has on shoes just like mine," she said, whispering out of the corner of her mouth, though no one was within thirty yards of us.

It was a typical California autumn day, with a hot sun and a cool breeze coming down from the Santa Cruz Mountains. We were at the school playground, our Saturday haunt. On Saturdays I kept my mind in neutral, watching the other Saturday people, the boys shooting baskets, the occasional joggers, the divorced fathers with young children. Without meaning to, sometimes I downshifted—what Professor Steed had said in the torts class and what on earth he had meant. And sometimes I ground the gears—how Ralph had betrayed me after all those years.

"Only she has on different socks," Stancy said. "See?" She gave my hand a jerk.

Standing on the platform of a swing was a little girl Stancy's age, being pushed by a man of about thirty-five with a lot of kinky graying hair. She had on tan Nikes like Stancy's and white socks. Stancy's socks were red. "Well, I prefer a bit of color around my feet," I said.

"Swing me," Stancy said. "Please." We were new in the dinky little university neighborhood, and she was desperate for friends. Soon the two swings were going full sway, but when our swing was forward, theirs was back. "Faster, Mom, please, faster," Stancy begged.

As the swings passed going up and back, Stancy cast looks of yearning at the little girl. She was like that, like me. When I imagined her future, I always saw her more loving than loved. She would be loyal and true and endlessly disappointed. I pushed as hard as I could. Soon we were almost even.

110

The little girl screamed, "Higher higher higher!" and the man began to pick up speed.

The little girls were flying higher and higher into the sky. When Stancy came down to the trough, she yelled, "Faster, faster!" but when she was at the end of the pendulum I heard her sharp intake of breath and then a squeal of fear. I decided to surrender.

"Enough," I said. "My arms are falling off." I walked off and propped myself against one of the long metal legs supporting the swings.

"Please, Mom, please!" Stancy yelled.

"How will I take notes if I don't have any arms?" I said. Stancy of course did not know what notes were, but the man did. I felt myself blush—talking to be overheard. "Let's go," I said. Although the swing had slowed, Stancy refused to get off until I said, "Constance. Now."

"We won," the little girl yelled.

"By a ligament," said the man, also talking to be overheard. When Stancy caught up with me, she wouldn't take my hand.

The next week I had to turn in my first paper for the legal writing course. I had not written anything in fifteen years, except a few vicious letters to Ralph, and I was almost paralyzed. I thought all the other students were brilliant and young and had just finished writing honors essays at Yale or Harvard and didn't have children but did have spouses who cooked their meals, washed their clothes, typed their papers, and went jogging for them. Whereas I was proof that Stanford Law School did not judge applicants by age, sex, or intelligence.

I called Ralph. "Can Stancy be with you this week?"

"Sorry, but I'm going to be out of town."

"Don't you mean we?" I said, rage suddenly flooding through me. "A little trip to Hawaii? Puerto Vallarta?" I could feel my eyes narrow, my lips turn inward hard against my teeth.

"Me alone," he answered. "Cleveland. Okay?"

"I wish I could go on a trip. But I can't. A—no money. B—Stancy to look after. C—I have to beat my brains out learning how to do something I hate so that in three years you can keep every penny you make all for yourself and your girl friend."

I could hear him sigh. "I'm sorry," he said. "You know I'm sorry about the split-up, Emily, but those things do happen. And talking the way you are certainly doesn't make me any sorrier. Try to get a hold of yourself. It isn't the end of the world. Tell Stancy I'll see her Sunday as usual."

Before I could get my answer organized, he had hung up. When I turned from the telephone, I saw Stancy in the doorway of her bedroom, looking hopeless as she always did when Ralph and I quarreled. "Don't look so morbid," I said as cheerfully as I could, though my heart was still pounding and my breath was short. "Just an ex-lover's quarrel. They always make up in court."

Stancy was lovely all week. While I went through eleven drafts in five days, she learned her multiplication-by-four all by herself, practicing aloud in her room. She wrote a paragraph about a book she had read and copied it out neatly without once asking for praise. One evening when Ralph called from Cleveland, I heard her saying I was doing very nicely in school.

And so on Friday night we celebrated by going to the Chinese restaurant that made Palo Alto's best pot-stickers, a Stancy favorite. We were standing at the door waiting for a table when Stancy pulled on the back of my jacket and said, "They're here." I thought she meant Ralph and his new lady friend. I faced away from the room.

"Did they see us?" I asked.

"I guess they don't remember us," Stancy said, and I turned back.

The little girl and the man from the swings were eating at a table a dozen steps from us. Stancy flushed and ducked her head. And so as the man and the little girl wiped their mouths and dropped their napkins on the table, I stared at them intently, willing them to remember us.

They did. When they got to where we stood, the man was smiling. "I see you got your arm sewed back on," he said.

"A miracle of modern surgery, though it's still a bit numb."

112

We all laughed. Stancy laughed loudest because she was most relieved. The man and the girl walked out the door, but as Stancy and I were congratulating ourselves for having made such a strong impression, the little girl reappeared. She was small and wiry and intense.

She said, "My name's Karen, and Daddy and I are going to the playground at two tomorrow. See ya." She ran off.

"Please, Mom," Stancy said, tugging on my arm.

I learned a great deal about them that Saturday and the following Saturdays, as Stancy and Karen swung first themselves and then each other and together climbed the iron igloo, Karen always in front. The father's name was Martin. He worked for a computer company in Silicon Valley. The mother lived thirty miles west in the mountains, and was, according to our new friend, "great." When divorce is mutually agreeable, the other person is always "great." Ralph was never great. The mother had Karen during the week, and Martin had her on the weekends. Though the arrangement had been in process not quite three months, Martin already was suffering the syndrome of the weekend father.

"I'm like a goddam hostess at a resort or on a cruise," he said one crisp October Saturday when we had known them about a month. "All I do is think up entertainments, novelties, distractions. I don't like it. I want it to be like she *lives* with me, not just *visits*. I want her to have friends in my neighborhood."

"It takes time," I said. "Stancy still hasn't any friends at school."

"Well, all I can say is, thank God for Stancy." He spread his arms across the back of the splintery bench. We looked at the girls. They were walking the cross-stud of the school fence, their arms stretched like wings. And then they both turned and jumped as far out as they could.

"And thank God for Karen," I said. "You can imagine how hard it's been on Stancy. The divorce, changing neighborhoods."

Then he grinned at me. "And thank God for the lady law-

yer." He leaned forward and chucked me on the arm. "One of
these days I'll have my own little software company—believe
me, I'm a hot property—and I'll need to buy me a lawyer." I
picked up his bantering tone.

"I sometimes wonder," I said, "what you computer types
who own the world used to do in, say, the eighteenth or nineteenth century when us verbal types were on top. I mean, did
you make harnesses for our horses and carriages, or did you
just plow?" When I heard his ringing laughter, I felt that my
humor was coming out of hibernation after eight dormant
months.

Soon the four of us seemed to take it for granted that we
would spend our Saturdays together. Mostly we met at the
park, but sometimes Martin planned a trip to the beach or to
the zoo in San Francisco. And sometimes we went for pot-
stickers.

Stancy made friends at her new school, but there was no
one she loved quite the way she loved Karen. Karen was
quick, bright, inventive, mischievous, and she never doubted
that Stancy would follow right behind, old Dog Tray ever
faithful. It hurt me sometimes to see just how adoring Stancy
was, but that was her nature and I could no more change it
than I could my own.

During the week, I learned to think like a lawyer, whatever
that is. Sometimes I listened with amazement and chagrin as
the professor and a student—a boy who maybe shaved once a
week whether he needed it or not, or a girl with the body of a
twelve-year-old—went lickety-split through a case, cutting
away the extraneous like so much suet. I never raised my
hand in class, and the sweet souls on the other side of the lec-
tern did not call on me, perhaps to avoid embarrassing the ad-
missions office.

It wasn't all bad. The other students did not address me as
ma'am or relinquish their chairs when I approached. Occasionally I even went to a party given by a student. The average age was twenty-three, and they all sat on the floor and
drank beer, smoked grass, and gossiped about the professors

and other students. I discovered that some of then envied the beardless boys and the anorectic girls as much as I did.

Martin was the only person I talked to anywhere near my own age. We bumped along behind the two girls, discussing computers, Stanford football, law school, and sometimes ourselves. Once Martin said he didn't think he would ever marry again, and I said I knew I wouldn't. He said he wouldn't because he had to admit he wasn't monogamous, and I said I wouldn't because I had to admit I was. He laughed and flipped my arm with his fingernails and said,

"You're a real nice lady, and you're pretty and funny, too."

"Thanks," I said. I felt hot with the pleasure of his words, and so I looked away to where the girls were playing. Karen was hanging by her knees from the topmost bar of the iron igloo and yelling for Stancy to try it. Stancy began to climb the rungs. I knew she would be frightened, but never refuse Karen. I stood up.

"Constance," I called, "Come here a minute." Gratefully she climbed down. "Do you need to go to the bathroom?" was all I could think to say. She was mortified, with Martin there.

The rains came early, and that meant snow on the slopes. Two winters ago, Ralph and I had rented a little cabin near Tahoe and spent the weekends there. At first I tried to ski with him, but one day I couldn't get the edge of my skis turned and I came straight down the hill going fifty and ended face forward in a snowbank. After that Stancy and I went cross-country while Ralph hot-dogged downhill with, as it turned out, the woman he left me for.

When Ralph called to say he wanted Stancy for the whole weekend, instead of just Sunday, so he could take her to Tahoe, I said,

"Stancy doesn't like downhill skiing, remember? Of course there is no reason for you to remember because you were off with the real skiers, rather than the family."

I heard him sigh. "She didn't like downhill because you didn't like downhill. This year she'll like it."

115

"You mean your girl friend will be a better model?" I said. "I don't think she ought to be with you and some woman in a little cabin with paper-thin walls. I mean, it may be okay to leave your family to satisfy your lust but it isn't all right to expose your child to it." The whiney shrillness of my voice seemed to echo from every corner of the room. I stood holding the phone, trembling, suddenly ashamed at how my self-pity, my self-righteousness, dominated me. I tried to lighten my tone. "Anyway, she has a friend she likes to be with on Saturdays."

Ralph said, "Which is it: the skiing, the morals, or the friend?"

"Whatever Stancy wants to do, Ralph," I said. "Ask her."

Stancy took the phone. I heard yes, yes, Karen, no, yes, Martin, I don't know their last name, yes, no. When she hung up I said, "Well?"

Her expression was blank. "He's going out of town this weekend, so I can't go over."

I gave her a big hug and a kiss on the forehead. "Karen would have been heartbroken," I said. She smiled complacently, and I suppose I did, too.

Martin had tickets for the Stanford-Arizona football game, the last home game of the year. He tried to explain the game to the girls—downs and the scrimmage line and what each player was supposed to do—until Karen said, "You're ruining the fun, Daddy." The girls took off down the steps. After that, they were only flashes of color disappearing into tunnels, clambering up the steps, shoving grown-ups aside, and then appearing suddenly for more money for more junk to eat.

While we watched the game—occasionally rising with the crowd to cheer, occasionally lamenting the bush-league play—we talked. We went all the way back to mothers and fathers and fingernail chewing (me) and bed-wetting (him). I found myself telling him about Ralph, my jealousy, my anger, my humiliation when I had to tell my parents and my friends about the breakup.

Martin said, "The worst of the pain is often just a bad case of embarrassment at not being loved."

116

"We married too young," I said. "It was time to move on." I was surprised to hear myself say that. "The trouble was, I didn't have any on to move to."

"Well, that's not going to be a problem," he said, patting me on the knee. And I thought perhaps that was true, that there might be something to move on to after all.

As we walked back to the car, dusk had begun to fall. Martin held Karen's hand and Karen held Stancy's.

Martin said, "Hey, the lady lawyer's unconnected," and then dropped his arm across my shoulder and rubbed his thumb below my ear. I felt myself tremble. It shocked me that this casual touch could so affect me.

"Pot-stickers, anyone?" I asked.

Karen shouted, "Daddy!" and the two girls began to dance.

"Oh, criminy," Martin said. "Next week, for sure."

The next week, Stancy went to the snow. When Ralph called that Wednesday, he said in a bitter tone, "What's the excuse this time?"

I said, "I don't want to quarrel with you. I feel good. My belly is flatter, my hair is shinier, my nails more shapely. It's up to Stancy."

"I won't be alone," he said.

"She might as well get used to the facts of life. They won't go away. If she wants to go with you and . . . Ruth, that's fine."

"Now that," he said, "is the old Emily."

"The very one . . ." I stopped. Instead of adding "you deserted," I finished with "who will call your daughter to the phone."

When I told Stancy her father wanted to take her skiing, she looked frightened. She said "What about Karen? What about Martin?"

"What about them?"

"Suppose Karen finds someone at the playground she likes better?" I knew what she meant: as Ralph had done on the vast playground of the snowy mountain.

I said, "She's your friend. Don't worry." She looked so doubtful, so sad, that I took her in my arms and kissed her.

117

"We're not just conveniences. They really like us. But it's up to you whether you go or not." I gave her a push toward the phone in the next room.

When she came back she said, "He said he'd die if another week went by without seeing me. I guess it'll be fun."

"You'll probably end up Olympics slalom champion."

I called Martin the following Friday and got his voice on the answering machine. I told the machine that Stancy would be gone for the weekend. I wondered if the machine was working and so I went by the playground the next day, but they weren't there.

Stancy had a good time. She said that Ruth had taught her how to snowplow and next time she was going to take her to the steeper slopes. She said Ralph did all the cooking and she and Ruth did the dishes. And then they all sat by the fire.

I decided I wasn't going to be jealous or angry. I only said, "What did you eat? Peanut butter sandwiches or did he venture out into fried eggs?" Stancy laughed. "Anyway, it's potstickers this Saturday."

We met Martin and Karen at the playground in the early afternoon the next Saturday. Stancy had been right—Karen had a new friend, a pudgy little girl named Mary. The three of them raced around the playground, Karen in the lead, then Stancy, and then Mary struggling behind, occasionally unleashing a frenetic giggle. Karen would laugh, too, and rush back to Mary.

"I don't know how long that will last," I said. "Three's a crowd." And I could have added Poor Stancy. Because I saw how it would be. Mary was jolly, new and not particularly in love. She was the challenge.

"She's the daughter of my friend," said Martin. "They went with us to Santa Cruz last weekend when you guys went to the snow."

"I didn't," I said. "You should have called. Stancy went off with her father."

"Oh, right," he said. "I hope you had a good week."

118

"Work," I said. "I've been fantasizing for days about pot-stickers."

"I don't think we can go with you this time," he said. "We have to pick up Mary's mother at the San Jose airport and take them back to Los Gatos."

"I didn't know Mary had a mother," I said. I tried to make a joke. "I mean, that she was your significant mother."

He laughed and flipped his fingernails against my shoulder. "She just moved back to this area last week."

I turned to look for the girls. On the far side of the swings, Karen whispered to Mary. Stancy stood apart, watching. "Constance, come here," I called. She ran to me and buried her head in my belly. I said, "I just wanted to tell you that you are the prettiest little girl I've ever seen." I turned to Martin. "We have to go now if we're going to beat the throngs to the pot-stickers. Tell Karen goodbye for us. And Mary."

He looked surprised. "Hey, you don't get rid of us that easily. We aren't going to let you just vanish. I'm going to need my lady lawyer for my new company. Right?" He ducked his head and looked at me closely.

"I'm sure they have plenty of lawyers in Los Gatos," I said. My smile felt like dried cereal around my mouth.

He drew me to him and held both me and Stancy in the circle of his arm. "We really care for you two," he said. "I mean, we really care."

When he released us, we walked away. At the corner, we turned to wave. By then Karen and Mary had rejoined Martin. Karen shouted, "See ya," and wheeled around and raced off again.

We decided to watch a PBS program that evening, and so after we had eaten our poached eggs, I gave Stancy some bubble soap and sent her to take a bath. When I finished washing dishes, I went into the bathroom and half-perched on the clothes hamper. Stancy was lying deep in the tub, only her head and shoulders visible above the drying bubbles. She said, "I don't think I'm Karen's best friend any more."

119

My pent-up fury exploded and spread like a brush fire. I said, "Good riddance. She's the kind of girl who likes to win friends and then throw them away. I've known plenty of people like that, people who pretend to care but don't really."

Stancy slid deeper into the tub, the tail ends of her hair soaking in the gray water. She looked so worried. After a moment she said, "They really cared, Mom. Honest. Martin said so." She watched me warily, hopefully.

It took me an instant, but finally I managed to relinquish my anger, my righteous, terrible, glorious anger. "You're right," I said. "Absolutely right. It was just one of those things. How come you're so smart, and you aren't even a lady law student?"

I motioned to her to stand up, and I took a big towel from the rack and wrapped it around her, and we held each other tight.

Lousy Moments

We met on the top floor of the old library. The students came one by one and stood silent and suspicious in the doorway. They shook the rain from their head-coverings—sombreros, knit caps, helmets, plastic shields—and then took chairs as far from me as the oval table allowed. For a minute or two, the only sound was the hollow pong the rain beat on the tiles of the roof. And then I read off their names: Bates, Connor, DeMoully, Dewey, Gowers, Ives . . . twenty-two hopefuls come to try their talents in a fiction-writing class at Stanford.

The first day always has an edge to it. The students are shopping around. They weigh the jokes, homework, coldness, competence, relevance, a dozen subtle factors that can't be named. I knew that at least two or three would decide against the course, that two or three more ought to. I described the work. It was a workshop and the subject matter was their stories. They would read aloud what they had written and the class would follow on photocopies. And then we would all comment, incisively, profoundly, gently. I told them the requirements: so many stories or, if you went in for long things, so many words per unit, plus participation in class and a tough skin.

A young man with a mass of hair like copper wire (Dewey?) asked, "Who does the word count, you or us?" A few students sniggered. I said,

"I feel the weight of the words." I held up my hand, weighing a manuscript. "I can estimate within seventy-five words out of ten thousand, so don't try to put me on with wide margins and big type." They gave me the easy laugh. People in special situations always get the easy laugh, politicians, octogenarians, teachers. A voice rose above the murmur.

"That makes me sick."

I found the source of the voice, a blond young man, thick ear-length hair, a soft feather of moustache, a delicate, fine mouth, and those light blue eyes that seem in a perpetual state of thrill. Probably a little older than the others. And handsome. And aggressive. It wasn't particularly unusual, I knew after seven years of teaching, to have someone throw down a challenge. Some male students are compelled to test the female teacher. I said, "I hate to make anyone sick this early in the quarter." I looked down the class roll. "Ives, is it?"

He sat low in his chair, balanced on his neck, rump, elbows, and heels. He said, "You make this sound like an engineering course. Mechanical engineering." A few students laughed. Others waited for my reaction. I said,

"As wicked as all that?"

"Creative work can't be quantified," he said. I shrugged—no argument there. "You can't count up words and expect to achieve a work of beauty." His voice was husky, strained, soft with tension.

"We're not talking about beauty, we're talking about students learning something about writing." I hadn't intended to be that tough, and so I hurried on, smiling. "The university is maybe the only place in the world where a person who wants to write can be supported and helped. But a lot of students take these so-called 'creative' courses because they think they're fun and games, a mick, an easy B. I don't want those students wasting my time or yours. So, everyone is going to turn in a respectable quantity if not quality of work. Okay?"

I didn't want to insist on agreement or capitulation, and so I paused only a moment. "Now I'd like to talk a little about technique, point of view, plot, tone, stuff like that. Art and beauty are all very well, but they'll never take the place of good old technique." The students laughed. By such harmless devices, I told myself, do I survive lousy moments.

Ives waited for me after class, and we walked together along the arcades of the inner quadrangle. "I know I was rude," he said. "It just means so much." I could see his moustache quiver.

"Let's just say you were decided or convinced. Don't worry."

"Writing is everything to me," he said.

I was struck by that and pleased. Most students say they want to be a writer, as if the role rather than the act enticed them. They dream of being the sage celebrity. He went on in a husky voice. "I know I have something in me, I know I have something to say, worth saying." We stopped and looked at each other. I noticed how pale his eyelashes were, how tight were the lines around his fierce eyes. I felt my own gaze waver. I knew he wanted an acknowledgment, an assurance. I wanted to say, How the hell do I know, I just work here.

"Even if you're immensely talented, it's still impossible to make a go of writing. Don't close off your options." I laughed, expecting to draw him into the comradely rue I felt for all those cursed with the longing. He turned and walked away.

At the next meeting I read the class a story by Isaac Babel. I had read that story aloud perhaps half a dozen times, but nonetheless by the last sentence—"But my heart, stained with bloodshed, grated and brimmed over"—I was choked with emotion, and my eyes brimmed over.

Dewey, the fellow with the wiry red hair, said, "Fantastic story. I read it a long time ago." They can't all be virgins. I asked him what made it fantastic. He thought for a moment, decided not to take a chance, and said, "No reason. It just is."

A young woman at the far end of the table—Marsh— wrapped her shiny brown hair around her neck and said, "Wasn't it awfully sort of simple?"

Ives said, "It was simple and strong and beautiful." Sitting on his neck, talking in that husky voice.

I said, "Good. Did you notice how the descriptive passages told you the narrator's moods were shifting?"

"No," he said. "Fortunately I did not notice that or anything like that. I merely responded to the whole story."

I laughed, to show he was joking. "First reading, it's probably expecting too much." I began to analyze the story. I selected passages, loaded with poignancy and irony, and I showed how the writer conveyed the mood without stating it.

Ives said, "Why do we have to cut it into little pieces like this? Why do we have to ruin it?"

"Ruin?" I repeated. "Trying to understand something is ruining it?"

"It's not that hard to understand."

"I mean, how it's made, how he made it. Anyway," I went on, another device to avoid the unpleasantness, "Babel is plenty tough. He can take it."

"Bullshit," he said.

We could hear the rain as it thudded against the greasy film of windows. Somewhere in the core of the building a door slammed. I said, "In a class in creative writing, the one absolute is, No clichés." The students laughed and relaxed, and I went on. "The theory is, if you understand the craft as a master practices it, you can learn to use it more effectively. And then after you've got the technique, maybe you can forget about it and concentrate on your own vision or whatever you want to convey." Ives slouched deeper in his chair, staring at nothing on the ceiling. I said, "Anyone who doesn't need to learn more about technique is wasting time in this class."

He did not appear for the next class, and I assumed he had heard the message. We read a Hemingway story and a Faulkner story. I talked about voice and authority and distance. Some of the students talked, too, or asked questions. At the fourth meeting we turned to a story written by a student. I criticized the work and so did they. One or two disagreed, politely, others offered suggestions or praise. Let me have students about me that are fat sleek-headed men and such as sleep o'nights.

Ives was back for the next meeting. I smiled at him—no hard feelings? He slid down in his chair. I distributed the story we were to hear and read. Its author was a big handsome fellow with a Southern California bronze. He always wore sweats and carried two tennis rackets in covers with "Stanford" stamped on them. The story was about young love, a pregnant girl, an abortion both refused. Instinctively you

124

knew your daughter was safe with the author, but the English language was not. He meant to be lyrical and was gaseous. He meant to show feeling and was maudlin. His intentions were great, his technique was rotten.

After he finished the reading and it was time for comments, I said, "Okay, who wants to shoot first?"

"Shoot to kill," said Ives, raking the crowd with a machine gun. Marsh wrapped her hair around her mouth to hide her laughter. I asked her what she thought of the story.

"I loved the language?" she asked. When the writing is unusual, no matter how bad, someone will love it. "That stuff about the eagles?" she explained.

I paged through the manuscript and found the section and read, "'Like four angry eagles trapped in a closet.'"

"See, it's concrete," she said. "Didn't you say we ought to be concrete?"

"But why four? Why eagles? Whose closet? Whose anger?"

A couple of hands went up, and we threw that around for a while. Dewey summed it up. "Not just concrete. Relevant."

Ives said, "You're ruining it for him. You're killing his story right before his eyes."

I turned to the tennis player. "Are we ruining it?"

He shrugged. "It wasn't worth anything anyway."

I said, "Listen. Here's what I like about your story. You care about people and decency and that's an essential if you're going to write. And you also care about language and try for effects. But you haven't learned control, restraint, yet. I like your story," I went on, liking it more and more. "I like it so well I want it to be better."

Ives stared straight ahead. The class was uninvolved, watching the struggle of the two power blocs. Power blocs? This boy? "So can we go on?" I asked him.

Ives was late for the next class. As we settled down, we talked and joked. It began to rain. The tennis player looked out at the rain and then stuck his tennis rackets in the trash basket, and we all laughed. Ives walked in, and we stopped laughing. We read a story by Janice Marsh in which everyone, including a horse, is in love with the heroine (who pulled her long hair under her chin). Late one night, early one morning, this immoderate fantasy—a longing, a hope—had struggled into words. It could happen to anyone. Ives raised his hand.

"Maybe it doesn't have what you would call the proper artistic distance, but it has real feeling. Do we have to tear it to shreds?"

I felt the heat rise to my eyes. With difficulty I forced a smile. "Oh, now, come on. We can't just sit around saying This is nice, this has real feeling, can we? We've got to think about it, analyze it, criticize it, because that's the way to improve. If you want to call that tearing your stories to shreds, then, okay, we're going to tear your stories to shreds."

"Like the Viet Nam village," he said. "We must destroy it in order to save it."

My peripheral vision told me a few heads nodded. One student said, "Right on," and Dewey, sitting close by, said, "Yeah, that's a good point."

I turned on him. "That is not a good point at all," I said, but for a moment I was at a loss. The analogy was so mindless, so far-fetched, yet on the surface it had force. Unscrambling someone else's metaphor is a useless task—by the time you succeed, everyone will have forgotten what you were going on about. I said, "Anyway, that's the way it's going to be. If it's too repulsive, perhaps you better not stay in the class. Now let's talk about the story." And we went back to Marsh's story, back to analysis, back to criticism.

When I returned to my office at five that afternoon to gather some books I wanted to look at at home, I found, half hidden by a thick red rug, a folded-up note that had been shoved under the door. "I intend to stay in the class because it provides me with the time to pursue my writing. It would be unconscionable for you to deprive me of that opportunity. Roland Ives."

I sat in my office a long time with the note spread open on my desk. The other offices went dark and the yellow lights came on all around the arcade. I thought of Ives, pictured the pale glow of his skin when he spoke, the faint flutter of his soft moustache, the bravado of his glance. He was a youth, really little more than a boy. And I, I asked myself, am I so rigid, authoritarian, easily threatened, petty that I can't tolerate dissent? Am I so easily undone?

But dissent can't be so uncivil and so mindless. That isn't dissent; it's assault. Rude. Bad manners. Was the difficulty his bad manners? Or was it his passion and commitment and confidence? I thought of Edith Mirrielees, who had taught at Stanford long ago, nurturing a rebellious Steinbeck. Maybe Ives was that one in a million who really could write, the one I ought to be nurturing. Maybe not. Probably not.

And there was the matter of the class. The other students paid their money, too. His outbursts might be good for him, good even to strengthen my character and develop my forbearance. But surely they weren't good for the class. Every meeting a bitter confrontation. A shambles.

And so I laid out all the elements, considered them, weighed them, in my imagination pursued their possibilities. And decided nothing, except to try to be patient, cool, rational.

The next time we met, it was one of those washed crisp days that make February the nicest month of the year in Northern California. I thought it was a good omen, and when I walked into the classroom and saw his bushy blond hair bunched along the back of his chair I made a vow: no more encounter groups, no egos flying around.

We read a story by the only black in the class, Clayton Gowers. It was about a white guy who is so in love with his Rolls Royce that he polishes it every night despite the importunings of a sexy young woman. Gowers read it in a thick ghetto cadence, his slurred words rolling from far back in his throat. I was fairly sure the story and the manner of the reading were a conscious performance.

"I don't dig it," said Dewey. He shook his copper curls until I expected to hear them jingle. "I mean, yes, distance and all, and you did it really well, but why'd you choose a white guy narrator?"

127

Gowers' cool eyes peered up through the narrow space between his mirror shades and the purple watch cap he wore low on his forehead. He said, "Black men don't drive no Rolls except pimps. You think they be less distance if he was a pimp?"

Dewey blushed so vivid a red that his light eyebrows stood out like Band-Aids on his forehead. I said, "Now, wait a second," and Gowers gave out an immense cackle, a metallic sound like pots and pans crashing on the floor.

"Come on, man," he said, "smile, smile, you supposed to smile. See, look, this is what they call fiction about fiction, you know, all that new stuff."

He began to expound on illusion and reality in the form of the black writer and the white protagonist, and he said that in his story even illusions had illusions, like the Rolls. What he said was complex and confusing and funny. Always before, he had seemed passive and suspicious. His story was his ticket into the group, and once he entered it, it at last became a group. We all felt it, and we were smiling. We talked about the ideas for a while—what is a fiction, whether realism is exhausted—and we finally suggested his intentions weren't clear enough and his language didn't sufficiently support the satire. He took it easily, gave a final cackle, and said, "I'm on some kind of heavy trip."

Ives said, "You don't have to put up with this shit. You don't have to write like the instructor wants you to."

"Goddam, here we go again," said Gowers. He drew back from the table, bored, not having any.

I said, "I don't much like this cerebral fiction, but if you want to do it, fine. I just want you to do it better." Ives was not looking at me, but I could see his profile, the stubborn, closed look, the eyelids pinched, the lips curled against his teeth.

"Art doesn't come from memorizing a bunch of shitty techniques," he said.

"That's just tiresome," I said.

"Maybe." He turned to face me, and as he spoke his voice

was no longer muffled, it was ringing and vibrato. "The only beauty, the only truth, the only good comes from feeling, not intellect at all. You're trying to make us into dry little professors."

"It takes both the head and the heart to do anything worthwhile," I said. "Alas, in this class we have to concentrate on the head because I can't do a damn thing about your heart."

The class laughed. Ives flushed and dropped his eyes. I felt suddenly depressed, as if the source of my energy had come unstoppered and been drained from me. I had taken advantage of my position and made him look foolish, and I knew that any attempt to right the wrong would worsen it.

When I went back to my office, I decided to have a talk with him, and I looked him up in the student directory. He lived at Crosley House, where a friend of mine was faculty fellow. I called my friend.

Yes, of course he knew Ives. It was a little hard not to, with all that intensity. Seems he had started out in physics, quit that and gone into psychology. A really fine student, when he was interested. Unfortunately, interest didn't seem to last long. At one point, he had had to drop out of school because his father died, something like that. And now he was back, more intense than ever. My friend had heard something about a period of hallucinogens, very brief—he was too smart for that. Then there was TM, or maybe he was a Christer. Anyway, you know the drill, all the excesses. Actually, my friend told me, Ives was a lot more interesting than that because he knew an awful lot about an awful lot.

"But odd," I said, "and difficult."

"When he gets a bee in his bonnet, he can be hard to handle."

"I guess I'm the bee. It seems I'm out to destroy art with a capital A."

"You ought to quit that," my friend said. "It isn't nice."

I rolled a piece of paper into my typewriter and wrote Ives a note: "If we talked about our differences, maybe we could find a better way to get along. Would you come by my office some day soon, please?"

He responded by staying away from class.

We were all happier without him. The talk was good-natured and helpful, and the students seemed involved in a common enterprise. Once, Dewey stopped by my chair on the way out of the room and said, "I was beginning to develop a chronic bellyache." We laughed and shared a look. In a funny way, Ives had brought us together. It was a good class.

Late one afternoon, when he had been absent for two weeks, Ives knocked on my office door. I assumed he was ready for our peace-making talk, and I smiled and gestured him into the room. But he handed me an envelope and walked away without crossing the threshold or uttering a word.

Inside the envelope was a manuscript, beautifully typed, held together by a black clamp. Under the clamp was a folded-up note: "When you count the words, you will find the prescribed number you demanded. I would be untrue to my feeling if I did not tell you that I know you are determined to destroy the young whose talents and purity of feeling you envy. You will not destroy me. Roland Ives."

My blood began to pound inside my skull, and I felt waves of emotion—anxiety, fury, fear—wash over me. Destroy the young? Had I read that? Whose talents you envy. That, too? You will not destroy me. Foolish, ridiculous. That self-important weasel, that ferret, that pig.

The flame of my feeling gradually died down. He was mad, of course, deranged. I should have seen that from the first, gotten rid of him the first day. A case of bad judgment on my part, a case of too much tolerance, or if that was putting too good a face on it, then a case of not wanting to concede defeat, of arrogance in thinking I could help him. Call it what you will—I should have done something right off.

I read the note again. Envy of the purity of feeling and the talent of the young. I sat at my desk and tried to understand exactly what he meant. Did that mean that he thought I was a failure? It is true, I said to myself, that I am no Austen, no

Chekhov, and to the extent that I once hoped I might be, I am a failure of sorts. But over the years I had published a good many pieces, and I was still writing and publishing, though I did not seem as driven as I once had been. More to the point, I was a damn good teacher, careful, fair, smart. I knew that, and that was all that mattered as far as Ives was concerned.

And so I threw the note in the trash basket and for the next half hour read through his manuscript. It was a reverie of a soldier during the lull between battles. It was bits and pieces of poems, dreams, philosophic musings, memories. There was passion in it, not forced, not pumped. But his writing exhibited faults I had attempted to steer the students away from—stasis, lack of distance, formlessness, excess, overly lyrical diction. I was grateful for its faults. I was grateful that it was no better than it was, no better than the general run of student writing.

But I did not trust my judgment, and the next day I took the manuscript to a colleague. "Read a few pages of this and tell me what you think."

When he brought it back to me ten minutes later, he gave me a quizzical look. "What's so difficult?"

"I've gotten negatively involved with the student, and I just wanted another opinion."

"Average. Lots of feeling. No form."

Ives showed up at the next meeting. Without a word, he began to distribute copies of his story.

"Wait," I said. "There's no point in our reading it unless you're prepared to get some comments from us." Dewey grinned and ducked his head. Gowers just grinned, hiding behind his shades. Ives looked straight ahead. He seemed to expect me to give in, to ease us into the reading, but I thought I'd let him sweat a little. "What about it?" He nodded. I said, "I didn't hear you."

"All right," he said. Before I could say that that was not enough, Dewey—nervous, sensitive—said,

"Then come on, let's have it." I nodded.

He began to read. He read first in a monotone so soft we

131

could barely hear him. But soon his voice quickened with emotion, and he read dramatically, passionately, shifting tone with each scene, each image. He rendered descriptive passages the way some poets read their poems, the voice rising to the end of each line as if the emotional throttle were left wide open for the next line. I felt the eyes of the students on me, but I kept my attention steadfast on the reading.

After he finished, he straightened his papers against the table top, carefully clamped them together, and slipped them into the canvas bag he had dropped alongside his chair. He hesitated, and I thought he might leave the room. Instead, he slid down in his chair until he was resting on his neck, his hands folded across his ribcage.

"Gowers," I said, "lead the way."

Gowers' glance shot toward me, under that hat, over those shades, intimate, knowing. More than that of the others—I knew and he knew—Ives would take his criticism.

"I guess that don't sound like no soldier wrote it."

Someone said, "You don't have to be a soldier to write about the war. Look at Stephen Crane."

Gowers answered, "The reader got to believe you been."

The class laughed. I never knew what Gowers' background was—I'd have guessed middle-class like the rest of the students—but he had developed to perfection the sardonic humor, the compressed syntax, the hair-trigger response of the ghetto.

"It isn't really about the war," said Dewey. "War is a metaphor." To Dewey everything was only metaphor. He was good-natured, outspoken, and sensitive, and the class loved to bait him. And so for a few minutes the other students had at him and his metaphors. As the talk crisscrossed the table, the students seemed not to notice Ives. They leaned forward to talk around him, as if he were only a pillar supporting the roof. And he ignored their ignoring of him.

I said, "I don't think we can solve any major philosophic issues today, so let's talk about this story."

Janice Marsh said, "I'm not sure about the language," and Gowers added,

132

"There sure were a lot of it."

"It was kind of heavy?" Marsh went on. "Thick?" Just briefly, the least gesture, unintended and instantly denied, Ives put his hand to his eyes. I said,

"You can learn to control that kind of thing. If you want to."

Ives came to life and sat up straight. He said, "I'm not interested in being fixated at the Hemingway level."

"Easy, man, be cool," Gowers said. Ives whirled on him.

"You do your thing," he said "or *her* thing," gesturing in my direction, "and I'll do mine." His quick gaze swept up the entire class.

"Okay, let's just talk about the story," I said.

Barely perceptibly, each student shifted to face Ives. And then they went after him. What did you mean by. . . ? What was the point of . . .? Why this, why the hell that? Was this a joke? Was that really *intentional?* If only he had responded, if only he had acknowledged them and their power to help or to hurt, they might have let up. But his only response was to go down in his chair, deeper, his arms folded, his head slightly cocked, signaling his contempt.

And so the attack intensified. It went beyond the tacit limits we had held as fair. One student complimented him for portraying his protagonist so consistently as pompous and self-righteous. Another professed to understand the piece as parody. Several selected out dreary or ludicrous phrases and, savoring each word, read them back to him.

From time to time I admonished them. "I liked that," I said to Gowers. "Aren't you being a little harsh?" Or I praised an image and once I said that sincerity of feeling was after all at the heart of the matter and who could doubt the sincerity?

I did not stop them. He was not a promising young writer, only an arrogant young man. Maybe, I thought, teachers in the arts are too soft—we let our students expend too much time and energy in a hopeless cause. Maybe if we were harder, the students would learn better and sooner their talents and limitations. I told myself that though the lesson was a hard one, perhaps it was in his best interests in the long run. Perhaps they could all learn from it. These thoughts, and others like them, moved across the front of my mind, but I knew even then, though more intensely later, that though baying silently, I was pack leader of the hounds.

When Ives at last straightened up, the students stopped speaking. He reached down alongside his chair for his book-bag, but he seemed not to have the will to lift it. He placed his hands flat on the table as if to steady himself. The pressure left white moons at the tips of his fingernails. I noticed how delicate his hands were, the delicate bones and veins pushing up against the soft white skin.

Marsh said, "Maybe you don't care what anyone else thinks."

"Enough," I said, raising my hand toward her like a traffic cop. "The class is over."

The students stood, gathered their papers and books, and put on their funny hats. They were flushed and slightly breathless, and they wore private inward looks.

Ives stood also, picked up his bookbag, and slung it over his shoulder. I said, "Wait a minute, please," and he seemed to require the greatest effort to bring his gaze around to mine. He looked skittish, like a child being punished, and yet defiant. His eyes, narrowed, peering through the pale lashes, seemed almost white with light. Without speaking, he turned away from me and flowed into the mass of students moving through the door.

Ives did not come back again, and none of the students ever mentioned him. The class went on to its end, a good class though somewhat subdued. About a month later, my friend from Ives's dormitory stopped me outside the office.

"Your boy quit school again," he said. "He decided there was nothing for him in academia."

"He has a point," I said. We smiled at each other and shook our heads.

We were standing almost exactly where Ives and I had stood the first day of the term, in the shadow of the university's inner quadrangle, within those thick sandstone walls where the university's cloistered life went on.

One Man's Poison

I am supposed to call Amelia Frame. More likely I will cross the street when I see her coming. I will stay away from the Birmingham Country Club on Tuesdays when she is there for the old ladies' mah-jongg. And when my telephone rings, I will answer it with great reluctance and perhaps in a phony voice so that I can say that I am not at home. She asked me to do her a favor, and I did it.

Amelia is a fine woman, with gay old-lady looks and stylish southern conversation, and she wears her wealth with easy comfort. She does neither good nor ill to anyone. An added quality, perhaps a vice—she is a little stupid, she will not leave well enough alone. See my son when you're in New York, Lucy dear, and tell me if he's drinking. I thought I could have told her, sure he's drinking. Then, now, and forever. But I liked her too well to want to rub her roughly on that old wound. And, to be honest, I had few enough friends in New York—I was stopping en route to a conference at the Connecticut headquarters of the insurance firm I worked for— and Carter Frame had been the best company I had ever had.

She gave me his address, and once there I didn't waste time on a telephone call. Suppose he didn't want to see me. Suppose he did. If I missed him or if I saw him, I wanted it be a matter of chance, certainly not his purpose.

The hotel doorman hailed me a cab, and six blocks away the taxi-driver, sly and self-satisfied with cunning, let me out. As I paid him and waited for my change, I looked around me, making a first effort to fix Carter in new surroundings.

All the houses on the street were identical, except that some had been reclaimed from decay by bright red or gun-metal gray doors and bronze Egyptian knockers, while the others had been left to peeling dingy white doors inset with glass etched in ragged lace curtains. An exotic neighborhood, where an art-dealer lives next door to a rooming house of indigents, a lawyer and his poet-wife are cheek-by-jowl with a street sweeper. And Carter.

His door was a bright Chinese red. It might as easily have been dingy white. He had grown up in a late-Victorian mansion on a street of mansions, a house in which his family had lived for nearly three-quarters of a century. And still imposing, still elegant. But he was one of privilege's sorriest products, and it was, I thought, surely by the grace of an impregnable fortress of trust funds that he still had the price of all that red paint. If you'd had my chances, baby, he used to say to me, you'd be wearing ruby buttons on your coat and diamonds on your blouse.

Carter himself answered my knock, and with that distinctly southern impulse I walked into his arms, saying his name, over and over, establishing between us the usual hypocrisy of utter gladness. One thing you can say for that hypocrisy, it buys you time, you can re-order yourself according to the tune of the moment. And Carter and I needed time—old lovers, eight years, and a marriage apiece later. We held hands a moment, let our arms swing between us, my handbag a ludicrous pendulum ticking off the awkward seconds.

"Come in, Lucy," he finally said in his heavy voice that seemed always to be voluptuously immersed in a cold. "You must be frozen. Let's warm you up with a drink."

I laughed. From his nineteenth year it had been that—warm up, cool off, perk up, calm down, end up, start out, wake up, settle down, get up, sit down, hurry up, slow down, always with a drink. We had toasted our engagement with a drink. It had ended with several. Who wouldn't laugh?

"Don't fret," he said. "I don't drink any more."

"No more," I said, "just as much." That was an old joke between us, and I expected recognition. What I got was a shake of my elbow.

"No more, no just as much, no nothing," he said. Space

136

opened between us, and feeling that I had presumed on quick-sand I let him guide me down the corridor.

As we entered the living room a young man in his middle twenties was setting a bottle down on the bar in a far corner. The bottle rocked precariously, and the young man's hand faltered after it. I was sorry to see him there, intruding in what I had come to think of as an encounter.

"I thought I'd just help myself," he said, looking abashed. He ducked his head and cajoled us with a soft baby smile.

"That's what it's there for," said Carter. He introduced us, and the young man, whose name was Billy, and I sat down across the coffee table from each other. On the table was a glass of what looked like some kind of cola and, seeing me see it, Carter mocked me with a deliberately silly grin.

"Lucy is here to spy on me," he said. "Nobody in Birmingham can bear the thought that I've stopped drinking. It meant too much to their pride."

"Don't fret," I said. "No one in Birmingham has the thought."

Carter gave me a quick open smile and said, "Hey, I thought I recognized you from somewhere." He turned to Billy. "If I'm not a drunk, the world isn't round, Birmingham isn't the Pittsburgh of the South, their grandfathers didn't own a thousand slaves, nothing they believe is true. Even Lucy. Especially Lucy? We were almost married once," he went on, talking to Billy, meaning me, "but I got drunk at the worst possible moment, and Lucy has far too much character to be forgiving. Right?"

I thought instantly of a half dozen smart responses, but somehow each seemed to lessen me, as if, accepting Carter's tone for this reunion, I had to lose whatever it was that had suddenly come to be at stake between us. I smiled socially, like a well-reared idiot, to shove him away. Yet if he wanted revenge, I understood that. I wanted a little myself.

New Year's Day in New Orleans for the Sugar Bowl game. Carter sprawled across the bed in his room at the St. Charles, the rich aroma of sweet vermouth—a desperate theft from our luncheon host—clinging to his mouth, the fear of failure, the recognition of inevitable failure, sprawled across his face. Wrapped in his bathrobe (Stewart tartan, I remembered), I wiped tears from his face and pressed cold cloths to his brow and the back of his neck until he went to sleep. I checked out of the hotel and went home as quietly as I could. To whom could I confess my humiliation?

Within a month Carter proved himself to himself by marrying a girl named Nettie Finney, mad to be married to a Frame at any cost—any Frame, and what a cost. She was one of those well-knit personalities who can't laugh in one room and cry in the next. When she cried, she cried all over the house. Every day and every place, until mercifully they left town, I got reports of Carter's drunkenness, told not in words but in her looks of anguish, begging pity and blame from me. The marriage lasted two years.

During those first months, I sometimes thought I'd put an ad in the society page, explaining that I had not been left at the altar, as cursed as all that. Instead, I behaved splendidly and listened in silence while my friends told me I was well out of it. Everyone dropped Carter. He was simply too heavy to carry.

And I did a deed that can be excused only by the brevity of its effect. I married a pleasant, innocent man who drank one drink before dinner and one drink after dinner on social occasions, and to whom every nuance had to be explained. I was as far away from Carter as I could get.

"That was quite a football game we didn't see that day, wasn't it?" I said.

Carter laughed. "Don't tell me what you want to drink," he said. "I remember."

He walked over to the mahogany bar built into the wall between a mass of bookshelves. The bar was backed by a sheet of antiqued glass crossed with clear glass shelves. On the shelves was a company of bottles, transparent, brown, green—a squat cognac, a lanky vermouth, a dozen or so of regulation size. The artillery rested on the bar itself—teak ice bucket, corkscrew of brass, four or five Steuben shot glasses, and several unidentified weapons of the nuclear age.

"That's quite a set-up," I said, "for a man who doesn't drink."

"And I'm quite a set-up," he replied without turning, "for a man who does drink." He came back across the room, bearing my martini. "Please do me the honor of looking at me straight at least for a moment." With his free hand, he pretended to pull up his eyelid. "The blue is blue, the white is white, there ain't no red."

I did look at him closely then. His eyes were clear, his face firm and lean, his skin a warm tan and smooth, his eagle's beak no more pinched and perched than it had ever been. And his whole face was still gentle and alert, but no longer flinching and vulnerable. I don't know what makes a person look dignified—the set of the lips, the ease of the shoulders, the repose of the hands—but whatever it is, I had to admit that Carter had it. And I had, at least for now, to believe no more, no just as much, no nothing.

"You always looked as if you had only been tippling champagne at a wedding," I said.

Carter turned angrily to the young man, not with a sudden recollection of his presence but as if he had been saving him for this purpose. "Lucy wanted to be the one to reform me. Carrie A. Nation. Joan of Arc. Eleanor Roosevelt. She resents the fact that it was done without her."

"You take terrible advantage," I said.

He sat down beside me on the sofa and took my hand, playing idly with my fingers as he spoke. "What can come of your being here? Can't you see how exposed I feel? If I still had to drink, wouldn't just your being here be the thing to cause it? I feel as if you're going to pack up and check out any minute and go back home. So I serve drinks to my friends. So I stock a good bar. It's my talisman, it means I trust myself. Is it the sheerest romantic nonsense to think you'd be a little proud of me instead of tearing me down?"

As he finished and yet continued to hold my hand, I didn't look at him, focusing rather on the tip of his ear, an empty vase behind him. I had not thought that I was tearing him down, or indeed ever had. I thought that I had tried to build him up. Failed but tried. I felt awkward and uncertain. Without the bottle in his hand, the foam on his lips, the whisky ruling even desire, was everything, as he had often promised it ultimately would be, "hunky-dory"? Except that I wasn't in it?

"All of us will be glad," I said.

"To hell with all of us," said Carter. "They don't care any more about me than I do about them. What about you?"

"I don't care any more than you do either," I said, and drank off my drink.

Carter scruffed my head in an old gesture of affection. "That deserves a small bonus," he said. He picked up my glass and reached across for Billy's.

"I ought to go," Billy said, and I shouted at him, yes, go, go. His soft face formed a soft smile. "It was bourbon on the rocks."

As Carter took our glasses to the bar, I tried to make talk with Billy, where he was from (Omaha), how he liked New York (fine), whether he found his job congenial (sure). He was a handsome man, lean and well-formed, yet hesitant and un-sure. Even as he made his monosyllabic answers, he appeared desperate to please and pretty sure he wouldn't. Carter had been reduced to dead weight for a friend. His redemption had come too late.

I needed to be wary. When something occupies your imagi-nation for a very long time, as Carter had occupied mine, when the central plot of a dominant fantasy ends always with a grand and vibrant crescendo, look out.

"Billy's only been in New York six months," said Carter from the bar.

"I didn't know anybody when I came," said Billy. "Every-body I know is through Carter. You ought not try to reform him." He looked at me earnestly.

"I'm not reforming him," I said. "He looks pretty good."

"Do I?" asked Carter. He brought our drinks and sat down in the chair beside the sofa, as bright as a bird, as mocking as a mockingbird.

"Carter knows everybody," Billy said. "I mean, he knows every kind of body."

140

"Not so," said Carter. "I've been saving myself for Lucy."

"Maybe you better spend yourself," I said. We were, for the first time since I had been there, in league, talking around as well as with this foolish boy, and I felt intrigued and at ease.

"No kidding," Billy went on, so serious, "there aren't many as good as Carter. Everybody around here respects him. Know what I mean? You people ought to leave him alone."

"We stayed to cheer," I said.

Carter's glance at me was as quick as a flick, curious, proud, amused. It was true that I had not respected Carter, but that was all I had lacked for him. Drunk or sober, he had always been able to touch me in a thousand subtle ways.

"When I came to this town," Billy went on, giving me as intense a look as anyone that soft could manage, "I had on a black suit shiny enough you could see yourself in it. Your undertaker wouldn't have been seen dead in it, even new. But I didn't even know it. I mean, I knew I had it on, but I didn't know I shouldn't. So who lends me the money to buy a new one? Who tells me where to get it? By God, who gets me the job to pay for it?"

"Could it possibly have been Carter Frame?" I asked.

"You bet. You people never ever appreciated him."

"Wrong," I said.

"I feel like a corpse," said Carter, "with everyone jostling for the first place on the mourner's bench."

"Well, I'd sure be there," said Billy. "Me and a couple dozen others."

Quickly, without another word, apparently the result of a gesture of Carter's hidden from me, Billy got to his feet. I realized he was terribly drunk. It was not so much that he was unsteady as that he seemed to expect to be. His eyes pieced out too carefully the posture of the chairs and table, and he took a too-deliberate bearing on the door. He turned to me with a slow awkwardness as if planning a final trumpet call. But he only nodded with a jerk and went out of the room.

At the front door he turned. "Okay if I come back around seven?"

141

"No," Carter said. "You can come at noon tomorrow if you like."

Why go on about the suggestion of seduction and the response it calls forth? These feelings are common and shared, and yet in a large sense incommunicable. For no one can speak with as many voices as a woman discovers at such times in herself, shouting, rasping, whispering, telling of desire and reluctance, of the fear of a failed composure and the hope of an understood look, those inner voices quarreling in the hallway, making impossible what should be easy, making probable what perhaps ought not to be at all. If only between the parlor and the boudoir there was no hallway.

When Carter returned to the room, he was smiling and expectant, as if waiting for some comment from me. And so I said, "Why on earth?"

"You don't see it?" he asked. He waited for me to answer, but I shook my head. "He doesn't remind you of anyone you once knew?"

"Don't be silly," I said. "You weren't a bit like that."

"On the surface, no. I never had a shiny black suit. But in the essentials, identical. Solving all his problems by getting too drunk to know they exist."

"You're a lot kinder to him than you ever were to yourself."

"He's down to his last friend, just as I was. It's not very pleasant to look around and find that there's nobody to catch you when you fall. So I like to think I'm there. It's a harmless enough vice, isn't it?"

Carter's look was incongruously comic, making fun of himself. He sat down beside me and took my hand again. "I like your hands. Always have. So sturdy. And I like your having come to see me. That's sturdy, too. And I even like your thinking that I get satisfaction out of cluttering my life with the likes of Billy. That's the sturdiest thing of all. True, but so what?"

I said, "Is that a challenge?"

"A clearing of the boards. To tell you to take me as you find me this time."

"Finish your story," I said.

142

"It was Bellevue," he said, "and it didn't cost me a nickel. That's one thing my family's money didn't buy me. One year ago June twelfth. One night I got rolled and didn't have any identification, and the cops threw me in the tank at Bellevue with all the other drunks. I thought women reached their peak in their twenties. You've gotten better."

"Go on."

"Have you ever been for five minutes in the alcoholic ward of a public hospital? I thought I was dead and there was after all a God because I was in hell. All those idiots yelling their lungs out, and I was yelling right along with them. You sons of bitches, you sons of bitches, over and over until they gave me a shot of something."

I waited for the rest, the hard-earned lesson, the moment of truth, the road out, the long cliché of struggle to victory, to self-respect, how he stayed sober. But Carter seemed to think he had said enough.

"I might have arranged that cure myself if I had known how effective it would be."

"You walked out too soon. When I'm not drunk . . . who knows?"

"At least a tiger," I said.

"I sometimes thought my appeal to you was simply that I was not a tiger."

The windows were growing dusky, and I felt evening as a threat, barring my escape. And I was not ready not to escape. The demand I felt him making was overbearing and insistent, and I wondered if it was quite personal and individual or only a desire for a general recognition.

"I've got to go," I said.

"Stay," he said. "Please stay. Here, I'll freshen your drink."

"No more," I said.

"No just as much?" he asked.

I stood up and slipped my arms into my coat. He said, "You haven't changed all that much. Still the little girl hoping her date will have the car so she won't have to sit in the back seat on the double date."

143

"I don't trust you now any more than I did when we were sixteen, and considerably less than when we were twenty-five."

He laughed, and I felt easier and happier. As I gathered my things, my handbag, my gloves, I realized I didn't want to lose him. I said, "Will you walk me back to my hotel? Your neighborhood's a little scary."

"This neighborhood is the whole world," he said. "It's anybody, it's everybody. I'm very happy here."

Outside it was dark and it was cold. Carter put his arm through mine, and we started down the street. We had gotten about a half block when one of the dingy white doors across the narrow street opened and a voice yelled:

"Wait up, wait up!"

I began to walk rapidly away, but Carter held me back. An elderly man plunged down the stairs and across the street. His gait was so awkward that he seemed to be walking on stilts. As he approached, I saw that he was shabby, thinly clothed, not steady on his feet, and not elderly either. He was a gaunt, unshaven drunk enveloped by the stale, rancid smell of old sweat and cheap gin.

"Hello, Pritchard," Carter said.

The man leaned into Carter's face, took his arm in a grip that seemed as much to steady himself as to hold Carter. He was, I thought, a cartoon of the indigent drunk.

"This is certainly a coincidence," he said. "I was winding up to go ask a favor of you, and here you are, just as though it was intended. Well, I mean I was at the window and I saw you passing. I wouldn't lie to you, Carter, not to you."

"I know you wouldn't," said Carter. "What's the favor?"

"Now, Carter," the man said, "if you say no I'll understand and turn away meek as a lamb. But here's this. My kid's sick, coughing like her shoes'll come up heels first through her head. What do I do? Listen to that poor baby breaking her mother's heart, not to mention mine but so what to that, or overcome my natural reticence and go ask the only real human being in my acquaintance if a small sum could be forth-

144

coming? For the medicine, mind, for the medicine. What do I do? Pride or love? You say."

"Love, always love," said Carter. "Of course you ask the favor."

Pritchard stood as tall as a cloud. "I humbly ask," he said. I assumed it was a ritual between them. Carter gazed at him a moment, rared back to look him full in the face as if judging the situation, and then extracted two five-dollar bills from his wallet.

"Before God," said Pritchard, "it's for the kid." He took the money with a jerk, turned, and lurched in his stiltlike walk down the street.

"All right, all right," said Carter, waving his hands in the air, "so he probably doesn't have a kid, probably not a wife. But couldn't you see how wild he is for a drink? You've not been there, you don't know. But I can tell you you're ready to rob or kill. You think your bones are going to burst out of your flesh. You think your tongue is flaking off and going to blow away. And you're just so grateful if somebody catches you."

"And you're there every time he falls?" I asked.

Carter laughed. "They go with me," he said. "I guess you ought to know that."

I took his arm. I could imagine that nightly as Carter passed, the ragged curtains were pulled back, the white doors opened, and out of them careened men like Pritchard, searching for the easy touch with a pocket full of money to pay for having escaped that fearful vision of himself.

"As long as the money holds out," I said.

At the revolving door of my hotel, I waited for Carter to ask to see me again. With a quick sense of deprivation, I felt that I had tarried too long, not checking out too soon this time but not checking in soon enough.

He pulled me aside. "You'd be a lot happier at my place. Ever think of getting stuck between floors in an elevator? Come on, let's argue about this over a drink."

Laughing with high expectancy, we went in the dim bar of the hotel, and Carter found us a table. We sat and held hands like tentative lovers, and the waiter brought our drinks, a martini for me, clear as water, water for Carter.

"Look at them," Carter said, motioning toward the long highly polished bar. I looked. Six of them lined up. Identical from the haircut to the cordovans. Young executive types emptied out of the glass buildings every evening. Behind the bar was a wall-sized mirror, marked off by rows of bottles. We could see their soft young faces between the necks of the bottles. They could see their own faces, which they did, from time to time, looking for something to stare at besides the glasses in their hands.

"This is the way it starts," said Carter. "Drop by for just one drink after a hateful day when what you did seemed pointless and you didn't even do it very well. Nobody was ever as nothing as you are. Take that kid, drinking from the shot glass. Alcoholic. It's written all over his face. Look at his puffy eyes, look at his skin, look at the flab under his jaw. One of these days I'll be at Bellevue watching the cops bring them in, and I'll remember that face. He'll be there sometime, sure as shooting. I never forget a face like that one."

I had been only half listening, thinking instead of what Carter and I seemed to be promising each other anew. But I finally heard the echo of his voice. "You're joking," I said. "You don't hang around at Bellevue to watch them bring in the drunks."

His attention swung back to me. He smiled. "Have another drink, Lucy. It'll help you fight off the tiger." His voice was tender and caressing.

I looked down at my empty glass, and I had a vision of myself as Carter saw me, some future time at Bellevue. I saw myself with slanted swollen eyes and a bruised cheek and skin shining with the oil of juniper berries. And I saw Carter bending over me with that happy inquiring glint burning bright in his eyes, searching out and memorizing every wound, the talisman of his own good fortune. At last he would be my true lover.

"No more," I said. "No just as much. No nothing."

146

Waiting

Usually visitors camp in the alcove a day or two and then disappear. Linda never knows whether the patient has died or the ailment has turned out to be so trivial—a broken arm, an appendectomy—that the drama has drained away. The lime-green plastic chairs with broken springs and slimy, mealy skin are hardly a pleasant place to spend the day.

The woman, though, has been there for four days, all day, every day, late into the evening, alone, like Linda. They have never spoken, but Linda has noted the well-tailored wool suits, the moderate display of jewelry and makeup, the courtesy and general cheeriness. May I sit here? Shall I move? Will this bother you? The woman appears to be in her late fifties. Linda is thirty-nine. Andy would be forty-two in less than a month. She knows he will probably not live to his birthday.

Linda feels a sudden lick of anger. She stands and walks quickly to the window overlooking the hospital parking lot, and she hangs on to the casement. The late afternoon sun glances off the tops of cars. Trees along the paths, pale with new leaf, sway in the wind. She can feel the commotion of the hospital behind her, the nurses, the orderlies, the flocks of interns and students chasing after the important doctors. Carefully, consciously, she relaxes her shoulders and back muscles. She breathes deeply.

She is ashamed of the blind anger aimed at everything and everyone. The woman in the alcove. The keeper of the motel where she is staying. Even the Gray Ladies dispensing charity and good will. She knows that no one is to blame. No one is at fault. A congenital malformation of the carotid artery. Unfor-

147

tunate genes. An aneurysm. A cerebral accident. They—the doctors, the nurses, the machines—are doing all they can to reverse the course, but they do not expect to succeed. She knows that. It is important to accept that. It is important not to deceive herself or others. It is important to be reasonable. That is keeping faith with what she and Andy have always valued. That is what they believe in.

She returns to the waiting alcove, sits down, and picks up her book from the large low table. Her eyes follow the lines. The woman says,

"Are you all right?" It is the first time she has spoken directly to Linda.

Linda says, "Oh, yes, thank you," and smiles mechanically.

The woman walks around the table. She has gray eyes and soft, well-kept skin. She says, "We're the regulars. Isn't it time we introduced ourselves?" She says her name. Marilyn something or other. Linda says her name.

Marilyn sits at a right angle to Linda and begins to talk. She explains that her son, a student at Stanford, has been in a terrible skiing accident. Someone skiing out of control had crashed into him and driven him into a tree. He had suffered a fractured skull. She says his condition is very serious. She says that she has flown in from Boston and that her older son will arrive that evening from London.

"You must not live in this area, either," she says. She gestures at the empty chairs.

"That's right," Linda says, "but not so far—Mendocino. It's about a hundred miles north." She glances at her watch. It is almost time to visit Andy. Marilyn grabs Linda's hand and begins to massage it energetically in both of hers.

"It's your husband, isn't it?" she asks.

Linda doesn't want this forced intimacy, this distraction. But she knows the woman means well and is suffering, too. And so she explains that Andy has had a stroke brought on by a congenital malformation of the carotid artery. She extricates her hand.

An orderly pushes a gurney past the alcove and backs it

through the swinging doors of the ward. Linda sees a form under the sheet, the head swathed in bandages, the mouth-hole gray with dampness. The woman says, "God tests us in mysterious ways."

"I think that must have been testing someone's driving skill," Linda says.

Marilyn looks at her sharply. "God gives us our cross and then the strength to bear it. He never gives us more than we can take, if we just believe."

Linda is surprised at this but does not respond. She picks up her book.

Marilyn won't be put off.

"I've been praying for you, every day, down in the hospital chapel. It'll be easier now I know your name." She laughs lightly. "I've had to say 'that woman in the tweed jacket' or 'that woman in the green silk shirt'—whatever you were wearing."

Linda has never seen the chapel, but she imagines that it is dark and cold. She imagines the woman on her knees, mur-muring, praying. She smiles and says, "I must be fairly far down on your list—you must spend a lot of time on your knees."

"You're way up there," the woman says. "I want to help you."

"Know any miracle workers?" Linda tries to laugh, but her throat compresses.

The woman says, "Jesus." She leans back in the chair and opens her arms wide, as though welcoming Linda to an em-brace. "Always when you least expect Him, and only when He's needed." Her eyes glint like polished silver. A sweet, childlike smile lights up her face. "He loves you."

Born again, thinks Linda. One of the primitive fanatics with a duty to convert the world. She feels again the rush of anger. She should have maintained her studied isolation, her sepa-rateness. She should have ignored the first overtures. Now she feels trapped by this woman with her clichés and her cheeriness.

She takes her handbag from the table and conjures up a distancing smile. "Excuse me," she says. "It's time for my afternoon visit." She knows she is a little early but she can hang around the nurses' station, weigh herself, use the bathroom.

"If I didn't have Jesus, I don't know how I could stand all this," the woman says. "You're a Christian, aren't you?"

"By birth, I guess, but not in any way that counts," says Linda.

"Any way counts," the woman says. "Jesus is glad whatever way."

"Look . . ." Linda begins. She fumbles for the woman's name. ". . . Marilyn, I won't discuss religion with you." She tries to soften what she has said. "Or anybody. I slam the door in the face of those Jehovah's Witnesses who come around."

"So do I," says Marilyn, grinning broadly. "They can't tell me how to be a Christian."

Linda has not been a believer since summer camp when she was fourteen. She doesn't remember exactly how it had come about, but one night after lights out she had begun to wonder how Jesus could raise the dead and walk on water. For the next few weeks she had thought about religion and the beliefs she had been taught in Sunday school. One evening she told the other campers that she was no longer a Christian. They had all been outraged, a few in tears. The counselor had sent for the camp minister to talk to her. And he had, for hours. We all have our occasional doubts, he said. My own favorite verse of the Bible is, I believe, oh Lord, help thou my unbelief.

When she resisted, his tone changed and he began to threaten her with damnation and then ostracism. She had held out. She wouldn't be bullied, and anyway everything he said made her realize more clearly that none of it made sense. At night, praying in loud voices, the girls had begged God to forgive her.

When she had gone home at the end of the camp session, she had told her parents that she didn't believe in the divinity of Jesus and didn't think she believed in God or immortality.

150

Her mother, a practical, conventional woman, had dismissed it with, That's ridiculous, you'll get over it. Do you believe? Linda had asked her father. No, he answered, smiling his ironic smile, but of course they say there are no atheists in foxholes, and I've never been in a foxhole. She had said, You wouldn't go back on your beliefs just out of fear? And he had said, What better reason?

Sometimes when sitting at the window and staring at the stars, she would suddenly see herself as only a speck of dust vanishing into that great nothingness. She would be filled with panic, and she would tell herself that perhaps she was wrong in not believing. Sometimes she would murmur, Help thou my unbelief. But she could not make sense of it. She had eventually come to accept her unbelief.

When her father lay dying of lung cancer, she had wanted to ask him, Is this the foxhole and have you gone back on your beliefs? But of course she had not dared.

"I bet no one can tell you how to be a Christian, either," says Marilyn.

"Well," Linda says. She pauses. She doesn't want to upset the woman. But aren't her beliefs important, too? Should she just swallow them and pretend to think what she didn't? "My case is different," she says. "I'm not a believer."

Marilyn smiles. "If you don't meet Jesus as your savior, you'll meet Him as your judge." Linda shrugs and moves toward the wards. "God bless," calls Marilyn. "We can talk later." No, we can't, thinks Linda.

When she pushes through the doors, her nostrils are assailed by the ward's peculiar odors—medicines, disinfectants, and an acrid smell she thinks is sickness itself. Intensive Care is at the far end of the corridor. As she threads her way through the gurneys and wheelchairs and respirators, she sees the flicker of television screens in the rooms and hears an occasional bark of laughter. The world goes on, she thinks.

Andy's room has three beds and a wall of machines and screens. There is always a nurse at the console, twirling knobs, reading the blips and dashes, adjusting the drips and drabs going into the bodies of the three men in the ward. This nurse is middle-aged, round, pink, mannish. When she sees Linda, she points her elbow at Andy's bed, as though Linda would not know which one he was.

Now is the moment Linda has dreaded. Although she has been in this room dozens of times in the last week, she always feels nauseated and dizzy. She reaches out to steady herself. Her hand falls on the back of a chair, and she manages to swing it toward the bed. She looks at Andy. His eyes are closed. Tubes protrude from his nose, from his arm, from under the sheet. He looks gray and wasted. The skin over his cheekbones is as tight as an old man's. His breath comes in jerks and hitches, and she knows it will smell like wet metal.

She takes Andy's hand in hers. Immediately he begins to milk her fingers, as though he knew she was there. Linda feels hope instantly surge through her. But she reminds herself that this action is instinctive, primordial. The doctors call it perseveration. There is nothing to base hope on. Andy does not even know she is in the room. He has not awakened from the coma since she had brought him in an ambulance to the hospital.

She thinks about the woman in the waiting alcove, and she pictures her in a chapel, praying for Andy. She remembers a cold March day in Florence when she and Andy had visited Santa Croce. In a dark, dank chapel they had seen a middle-aged woman mumbling and banging her head on a sarcophagous that held the remains of a saint. A little stream of blood flowed down her cheeks. Back at the *pensione*, Linda had expressed her disgust at the simple-mindedness, but Andy had said he found something touching and enviable in that kind of faith.

That is Andy's way. Rational, understanding, forgiving of people with different views. She knows that she is not naturally forgiving or tolerant. If she were religious, she would be a Savonarola, insisting on the true faith. Without Andy, she would probably have become a fascist or a communist. A liberal fascist, he once teased her, a furious moderate with an iron fist. She lifts his hand to her lips and kisses it.

152

Something is going on at the console. The nurse presses a button and almost immediately a man in a green tunic appears and rushes to the bed next to Andy's. The nurse looks at Linda and says "Git," in a furious voice, as though Linda is the root of the trouble.

Linda goes out into the corridor. She sees Dr. Holmes standing at the nurses' station, leaning over the counter toward a pretty red-headed nurse. He is Andy's doctor. Their doctor in Mendocino had said Holmes was the best neurologist he knew. Linda wonders what it means to be the best in a hopeless situation. Does it mean he is most accurate in his description of disaster?

"I left a call this morning," she says as she approaches, "but I guess you've been busy."

"All the world seems sick today," he says. "And I knew I'd see you here." He is wearing the doctor's studied look of concern and reassurance. He is a large-boned, pudgy man, perhaps a jock gone to fat.

"Can you tell me anything?" she asks.

"There's no change that I can detect," he says.

"These things must run a course," she says. "Do you think you'll ever know more?" She knows her voice is challenging, but she cannot control it.

Holmes's expression sours. He leans back against the counter and braces himself on his elbows so that his belly swells toward her. "We're doing all we can."

And again she is furious. Is flirting with a nurse all he can do? "And what exactly is that?" she asks.

Holmes stands straight and leans toward her. "If you want to consult another doctor, be my guest." He smiles a hostile smile and waits.

They stare at each other for a moment. She feels as though she is standing on a precipice of anguish, fury, perhaps tears. She holds herself rigid. It is not his fault, she reminds herself. It is wrong to blame him because he can do nothing in a hopeless case. "Sorry," she says.

She turns away. She decides to walk down the inner staircase to avoid the waiting room.

153

It is almost six o'clock when she gets back to her motel. She decides she will call home before she goes next door to the little café for her nightly omelette or cheeseburger. First, though, she goes to the refrigerator under the dressing-table mirror and takes out a bottle of white wine. This is ritual. Every night when Andy had come home from his law office, they had sipped wine and gone over the events of the day. Her days were less exciting—chauffeuring the children, volunteer work, her book binding—but he seemed to want to hear about them as much as she did his cases, his business dealings, the town's politics. Today, she would have told him about her encounter with Marilyn.

Her mother answers the telephone. Her mother says, "Linda, Lindy, darling. How is everything—besides ghastly, of course." Her mother's voice, a rich contralto, sounds warm and strong.

"About the same," Linda says.

Her mother says, "I'd rather it were I than Andy." She has said this every night, and Linda knows it has never been true. Her mother is sixty-eight and full of health and energy. She will hold tenaciously to life deep into her nineties. She still runs the boutique she bought after Linda's father died, still plays tournament bridge twice a week, still drives into San Francisco once a month for the opera or the theater. "But how are you, my darling baby?" her mother asks.

"I'm all right," she says. "I'm fine."

"You're fantastic," says her mother, "you're unbelievable, you're so strong."

"Tell me another way to be," says Linda, "and I'll try it. Let me speak to the girls now."

Diana comes to the telephone first. She is ten and the older. Linda says, "What happened in school? Tell me everything, just as though I were home."

"How's Daddy? Is Daddy any better?"

For a second Linda thinks how easy it would be to say yes, Daddy is better. To bring happiness, if only for a moment. Perhaps even to believe it herself. Linda says. "The doctor says he's the same."

"Is he going to die?" asks Diana.

Linda can hear her mother protesting in the background. "I don't know," she says.

"Is that the truth?" Diana asks.

"You know I don't lie to you," says Linda.

"Give me the phone," she hears her mother say. Diana holds onto it.

"Do you *think* he is going to die?" she asks.

Linda pauses. "Yes, but I don't know it."

"Grandma says that if we pray to God, then Daddy will get well. But you don't believe in God, do you?"

"No," says Linda, "but in a way I envy those who do."

"Why?" asks Diana.

Linda takes a deep breath. "Because it would be wonderful to think that even if Daddy dies, we wouldn't really lose him."

"Grandma says we'll all be together in heaven."

Linda feels a little spurt of anger at her mother. "Well, she has a right to her opinion," she says. "Let me talk to Janie now."

Janie is six years old. When she comes to the telephone she immediately says, "I don't believe in God either. It's dumb to believe in God."

"Now wait a minute," says Linda, laughing. "Don't go feeling better than other people just because you don't believe the same things they do."

"I don't feel better," Janie says quickly, "but I'm as good. I'm as good as Diana, but Grandma lets her stay up later than me. That isn't fair, is it?"

"First," Linda says, "Grandma is the boss—just be grateful she's there. Second, Diana is older and therefore doesn't need quite as much sleep. Third, I miss you like crazy."

"I miss you, too. When are you coming home?"

"Soon, probably," Linda answers. When she realizes the implications of that "soon," she feels weak, overwhelmed. "Not for a while," she manages to say.

Back on the telephone, Linda's mother says, "Sometimes I wonder if you have good sense. Teaching those little things not to believe in God at a time like this." Her voice is prim-lipped, exasperated.

"This is the only time that matters. The rest of the time it's easy enough not to believe. This is the foxhole."

"You've always done that to them," her mother says. "You wouldn't let them believe in Santa Claus or the tooth fairy or anything."

Linda laughs out loud. "Santa Claus, the tooth fairy, and God. How about the stork?"

"Don't try to be so smart," says her mother. "You know what I mean. These little things need God, with their father dying . . ."

At these words, all the images the talk had pushed aside come rushing back—the hospital, the tubes, Andy melting into death. And suddenly Linda feels a deep shudder of fear and exposure, and she wants desperately for her mother to be there with her, to hold her, to reassure her—as she had when Linda was a small child and frightened in the night—that there was no death because there was a marvelous bright place called heaven where everything was wonderful. Remembering the warm breath of her mother lying beside her in the bed, the warmth of her mother's arms around her, Linda cannot speak for a moment.

"Honey?" her mother says. "Darling? I'm so sorry. Do you want me to come down there? Shall I get someone to stay with the girls? I could drive down tonight."

Linda controls her sobs. "No," she says, "I want you to be with them." And then a shriek of laughter breaks like lightning through her sobs. "They don't put their trust in God, but at least they can trust their grandmother."

By the time Linda gets back to the hospital, the corridors are almost deserted. When she steps off the escalator on the third floor, she sees Marilyn in her usual place in the alcove. Her face is buried in her hands. A man with a stethoscope around his neck stands with his hand on her shoulder. A nurse hovers nearby. Linda understands that Marilyn's son is dead.

She steps back behind the corner of the wall. She wants to avoid Marilyn. She doesn't want this encounter. What could

156

she say? Isn't she exactly the wrong person at this time? She has no comforting Christian homilies. And she doesn't need this—she has her own troubles. She decides to slip away to the down escalator and come up the inner stairway to the ward.

As she turns away, she hears her name called by the nurse. The regulars—everybody knows the regulars. The nurse walks over to her.

"Would you mind . . .?" the nurse begins.

"No, I'm sorry." She looks toward the alcove. The doctor has taken his hand from Marilyn's shoulder and is already inching away. It is his duty to offer sympathy. It is his duty to move on. Perhaps it is her duty to stay. "All right," she says just as Marilyn looks toward her. She walks to the alcove and sits beside Marilyn in one of the dank chairs. Marilyn looks old and fragile. Her cheeks are marked with shiny streaks like snail tracks.

"It's over," she says and hunches down in her chair and presses her fists into her eyes.

Linda sits beside Marilyn and puts her arm over Marilyn's shoulders. Soon Marilyn's tears subside, and she sits twisting her fingers.

Linda glances around. Both the doctor and the nurse have disappeared. Down the corridor, two young men and a young woman, all in green hospital smocks, are howling with laughter. One is gesturing with his stethoscope, demonstrating something. A sleepy janitor leans against a wall, hanging on to his mop. Now Linda must say something. But what can she say about a boy she never knew to a woman whose beliefs are so different from hers? Platitudes, inanities, false comfort. What will people say to her when Andy dies? He was a good, kind, intelligent man. As though words could compensate.

"Is there anything I can do?" she asks. "Anyone I can call?"

"My son will be here soon. My other son." Marilyn's face collapses. "I just wish I understood," she almost shouts. "Why not take my life? Why not some old man who has to be fed with a spoon? How could God do this? How could He be so cruel?" Her voice is bitter, angry. She stands up, trembling.

"I want to go into the chapel," she says. "I'm afraid. It's so hard to accept. Please come with me." Her voice is urgent.

Linda does not want to go into the chapel. If she doesn't hurry, the nurses won't let her in to see Andy. Of course, he will not know she is there. And wouldn't he want her to help this grieving woman?

The chapel is empty. A yellowish globe hanging from the high ceiling lights the rows of polished benches and the dark concrete floor. At the front is a table with a white cloth and a small crucifix flanked by two lighted candles. Marilyn leads them to the front row.

Linda watches as Marilyn rocks back and forth and weeps into shredded tissues. After a few minutes Marilyn stops crying. Her head drops forward and she sits immobile for a moment. Then she turns to Linda. Her eyes are like molten silver. "My boy has gone to God," she says. "God decided He wanted him. His will be done."

Linda wonders if Marilyn really believes that her son's death is somehow the will of God. Has she forgotten the accident, the tree, the crazy exhibitionist flying down the mountain, the uselessness, her own anger? Has believing that God had a purpose brought her comfort? Has it lessened the pain and made the death more acceptable? Is this what belief comes to?

Marilyn reaches over and takes Linda's hand and pulls her down to an adjacent footstool. "Please pray with me," she says. Linda kneels beside Marilyn. She feels the chill of the room and gathers her sweater about her. She senses that Marilyn is watching her and so she lowers her head.

As she kneels in the darkened room, listening as Marilyn mumbles a prayer, she thinks of Andy. She sees his wasted face, the tubes, the attentive nurse working at her dials. She knows that he will die. The doctors have said as much. If she could believe it was all God's will, that there was a mysterious meaning, a purpose, would she, too, be comforted? God watching and caring. Not accident, not chance, not just bad luck and bad genes. If she could be as trusting as Marilyn, would that help her to accept Andy's death and bear her pain and fear and anger? Perhaps she could stop her unbelieving. She closes her eyes. For a moment, she feels small and soft, as helpless as a child.

Someone opens the door of the chapel and a man's voice whispers, "Mother?" Marilyn stands and goes to him. He folds her in his arms, and they hold each other. And then they both kneel at the back of the chapel.

Linda straightens up. That's enough, she says to herself. She has done her duty to Marilyn. Now she wants to be with Andy. She rises and moves in the shadows to the door. She hopes the nurse will let her in to see Andy even though it is past visiting hours. She takes the escalator to the third floor.

When she pushes through the swinging doors of the ward, she sees the floor nurse and Dr. Holmes talking outside Intensive Care. When they glance up and see her, they stop speaking. They start toward her. She walks to meet them, repeating to herself congenital malformation, genes, aneurysm, cerebral accident.